# THE
# COLDEST
# HOE Ever

*How Bad Can a Good Girl Get?*

# CORNELIA SMITH

**The Coldest Hoe Ever**

Copyright © 2015 by Cornelia Smith

All Rights Reserved

# Other Titles by Cornelia Smith

If you're new to reading Cornelia Smith books. Here's a great place to start. Pick-A-Series below:

➢ **Sleeping in Sin: The Lesson:** <u>Sleeping in Sin: The Lesson - Kindle edition by Smith, Cornelia. Literature & Fiction Kindle eBooks @ Amazon.com.</u>

➢ **The Black Butterfly: A Damaged Soul:** <u>The BlacK Butterfly: A Damaged Soul: Smith, Cornelia, Lancaster, Eeva: 9781946221100: Amazon.com: Books</u>

## This is an advance notice:

**The material that you are about to read is very sexual and provocative. It could be very alarming and offensive to individuals who do not believe in minors/young adults being sexually active.**

Also: To Author Cornelia Smith die hard readers A.K.A. Butterflies, this is a RE-RELEASE edit and improved book.

www.thebookplug.com

# 1

Emerson walked into a house full of half-naked women scattered all over his seating area. Jasmine's Child's *Free* softly played on the Sony radio system. The Brazilian breeze candles were burned down low and empty Ace of Spades bottles decorated the coffee table.

"Get your ass up, Brianna!" Emerson's Jordan smashed into Brianna's ass, and it bounced back like Jell-O.

"Why you got all these hoes in my house?" Brianna wiped the cold out of her eyes.

"Calm down, damn. It's not that serious!" she responded. Frustrated with Brianna's tone, Emerson swiped her across the mouth with his backhand.

"Who the fuck you think you talking to, bitch?" Before Brianna could give a response, Emerson snatched her up by her 28" Brazilian weave and tossed her into the wall.

"Bitch, you know I don't even play them games. You better watch who you talking to!" Emerson's grip around Brianna's neck tightened. "Why the fuck are these hoes in my house, Brianna?"

"I thought you were gone out of town for the weekend. I just wanted to have a girl's night with my girls," she gasped with little to no air to breathe.

"I don't like people all in my personal space where I lay my head, especially not hoes and you know this shit!" Emerson yelled as he smashed Brianna's head into the wall.

"Who the fuck are you calling a hoe, motherfucker?" Jordan popped up from the sofa.

"I'm talking about y'all hoes." Emerson charged at Jordan with his fist clenched tight.

"Bitch, I wish you would put your hands on me. It will be the last time you ever put your hands on a female." Emerson stopped in his tracks as Jordan grabbed her Levi jeans off the floor and slid them over her round ass.

"She wouldn't have to bring company to your house if you let her out more, instead of keeping her cooped up in these four walls." Jordan searched the sofas for her clutch and Emerson turned around to Brianna and pounded his fist into her left eye.

"So, bitch, I keep you locked down? So, that's what

You're telling hoes now?" Furious, Emerson dragged Brianna by her hair and down the hall toward the staircase.

"Please Emerson, do not hit her!" Brianna's younger sister Skylar cried out.

"That's what fuck niggas do, Skylar. Don't worry I'm calling the police." Jordan picked up her Galaxy and pretended to call the police.

"Please don't, Jordan, it's okay. I'm okay," Brianna yelled out as she struggled to untighten Emerson's grip around her hair.

"Bitch, if this hoe calls the police on me, I'm putting your black ass out my shit." Emerson let loose of Brianna's hair and shoved her head into the stairs. Before he stormed up the stairs, he screamed out, "Get that hoe out my house, Brianna, before I fuck her up!"

"Jordan just leave. Here is some cab fare." Brianna snatched her Michael Kors bag off the floor and pulled out a hundred, handing it to Jordan. She refused it. "I don't want him to hurt you, Jordan. Just leave."

Jordan's emerald contacts watered as she stared into Brianna's light brown eyes, shaking her head side to side.

"You're pathetic, you know that?" Tears gushed down Brianna's face. For thirty seconds, she sobbed silently then finally she blubbered out, "He just had a bad day at work, Jordan. You'll never understand what a man is like until you get one of your own."

"No, I understand men, Brianna, I just don't understand dogs." Jordan snatched her clutch off the arm of the sofa and stormed out the door.

"Go after her, Brianna," Skylar said, pointing to the door. "No, you don't know Jordan like I do. You got to let her cool off or there will be no reasoning with her. You can sleep in the guest room. I'll take you home in the morning." Brianna said before she exited the living room.

Jordan tried to stop the tears from flowing but they ignored her demand. She couldn't understand why she was so surprised at Brianna's actions since it wasn't the first-time Brianna had taken Emerson's side over hers.

"Brianna don't ever have to worry about me coming around her dumb ass no more," Jordan murmured as she walked  down the long street with limited light poles.

*Bump, bump, bump.*

"Well, stop and give me a ride if you gon' blow," Jordan babbled as she continued her quest to the nearest Train station, hoping she would find a cab there. *Bump, bump.*

"Do you need a ride, sweet thing?" An African with an heavy accent asked Jordan. She eyed her surroundings to see if she could see anyone, but the night was ghost. She took another look at the African, trying to spot a sign of craziness, but she found none.

"*What the hell*," she thought, jumping in the silver 2011 Dodge Durango truck.

"Where to, my queen?" the African asked, taking a glimpse at Jordan's apple round breast.

"You can take me to the train station. I'll find me a cab from there." Jordan buckled herself in her seat belt.

"Where do you live? I can take you home, it's not a problem."

"Oh, it's okay, I stay in Metro Atlanta. It's a little ride from here."

"It's fine, I'll take you," the African insisted before

driving off. As Jordan responded, "Thanks," she caught the African staring at her round apples. The morning was young, and the cool breeze had hardened Jordan's nipples through her white tank, and Mr. African couldn't keep his eyes off Jordan's hard fruit.

"So, what's a beautiful girl like yourself doing out here

in this lonely world all by yourself?" The stranger asked, gliding his wandering hand on Jordan thigh.

"I got into a fight with a friend," Jordan snapped, aggressively throwing the African hand off her thigh.

"I understand. So, where is your man, beautiful?"

Jordan inhaled the horrible cologne the African was wearing, and immediately got frustrated.

"I don't have one," she answered with an attitude.

The driver smiled and said, "That's good for me. So, can I make you happy?" Jordan knew that was slang for *Can I buy some pussy?* So, she rolled her eyes at the African and answered, "You couldn't afford me if I gave you the opportunity."

"How much you want, beautiful?" Finally, he rubbed

Jordan's nipple and then licked his tongue.

"I'll make it worth your while, I promise."

"And what makes you think that will please me?"

Jordan flung his hand off her breast andturned her attention towards the window so she wouldn't have to watch him lust for her. Shortly after, she spotted a cab at the gas station the two were passing and said, "You can

let me out here. I see an old friend." The African pulled over to the curb and ask, "Can I call you sometime?"

"Nah, I'm not looking for a man right now, but thanks for the lift."

# 2

---

*Speeding down the road, and my head out of control, Cause I'm thinking about you all the way home Got a long way to ride.*

"**U**gh, fuck, quit calling me!" Jordan was beginning to hate one of her favorite Tamar songs. Her phone had been ringing for ten minutes straight.

*Speeding down the road, and my head out of control Cause I'm thinking about you all the way home Got a long way to ride.*

Giving up on sleep, Jordan finally stuck her head out from under the pillow to take a glance at her clock. *1:45* P.M. Then she eyed her ringing phone.

"What do you want Brianna?" Jordan answered.

"Don't hang up. I just wanted to say I'm sorry. Please don't be mad at me." Jordan rolled her eyes as if Brianna could see her.

"I'm not mad, and to prove it, I'm ending this phone call." Jordan was disgusted with Brianna's fake whimpering. She always used crying to get her way.

*Speeding down the road, and my head out of control Cause I'm thinking about you all the way home Got a long way to ride.*

"Quit calling my phone, Brianna! I'm through with your dumb ass. You always been boy crazy, and frankly, I'm through with it." Jordan stumbled to the bathroom to wash the cold out of her eyes.

Before she could press the end button on Brianna, she blurted out, "Skylar was killed in a car accident this morning, Jordan! I know I fucked up, but I need you." Brianna broke down, whimpering hard and Jordan's heart dropped to her gut.

"What'd you say?" Jordan whispered with the little breath she had to talk.

"You heard me right. Skylar was killed in an accident this morning. She was hit by an eighteen-wheeler." Jordan's bottom fell flat to the bathroom floor. It felt surreal. She and Skylar were just laughing and sipping Ace of Spades last night.

"Why was she driving? Brianna, you know she can't even drive!" Jordan cried out.

"I told her I would take her home, but she didn't want to wait for me. When I got up this morning she was gone in my car." Jordan's eyes rained salty tears.

"All you had to do was get your black ass up to take her home and you couldn't even do that! Lying up under that buster-ass nigga. Fuck!" Jordan broke down, crying with Brianna. She and Skylar were like sisters.

Jordan and Brianna had been best friends since they were in the fifth grade, and the two of them looked after Skylar like she was their child since Brianna's mother had a strong love for cocaine.

"I need you, Jordan. I'm not going to make it. I swear I can't take this shit. It hurts so bad..." Jordan listened to Brianna cry, and she knew she

wasn't playing around this time. Skylar was the only family Brianna had outside her drug-addict mother Roxanne.

"I'll be over there in a minute…just give me a minute." Jordan never got a response from Brianna, she only got whimpering. Brianna was out of it, and it was nothing Jordan could fix over the phone.

*Knock, bang, whack, knock.*

"It's me, Brianna, open up!" Jordan screamed as she beat down the door, whack, knock. "Come in, Jordan," Emerson said as soon as he opened the door. "She's in the kitchen. She hasn't stopped crying since she got the news." Jordan rolled her emerald contacts and stormed passed Emerson.

"Brianna come on now. You got to pull it together, baby." Jordan wrapped her arms around Brianna's body and kissed her on the cheeks.

"Stop crying, friend, don't cry." Jordan sniveled. "Did she have insurance?" Slowly Brianna nodded her head *no*.

"Well come on, we got to get it together, even if it's just until we get her buried."

"Come on Brianna, we got to try to get the money up to bury her, pull it together." Jordan pulled Brianna to her feet and walked her to the kitchen table.

"Oh, I already told her I'll take care of the funeral. She doesn't have to worry about that." The sound of Emerson's voice instantly irritated

Jordan and her look showed the disgust, but she couldn't ignore the fact that Emerson was being considerate at the right time.

"Thank you." Jordan swallowed her pride and said with an attitude.

"Oh, you don't have to thank me. That's my woman, I'm always on her right hip when she needs me." Jordan couldn't shake the feeling that told her Emerson was full of shit, but she just ignored the feeling for the time being.

"Do Roxanne know, Brianna?" Brianna's light brown eyes locked in with Jordan's emerald ones.

"No, I haven't been able to reach her," Brianna answered, wiping her tears.

"Well, you just gon' have to fly to Alabama to get her because we can't bury Skylar without her mother even knowing she dead."

"I know," Brianna said, sobbing and sniffling.

"Shit, if she cared her ass would be here. Brianna not about to go to no damn Alabama. Who the hell's gonna get Skylar's funeral together?" Emerson spat. If Jordan's frown could kill, Emerson would be dead. She so badly wanted to be the bigger person for Brianna, but Emerson just pushed her worst nerves.

"What the hell you talking about, Emerson? That's Skylar's mother and no matter what she did, Skylar loved her dearly. We're not about to bury Skylar without Roxanne even knowing that she's dead." Brianna took one look at Jordan, and she knew it was about to get heated. Jordan never bit her tongue, no matter the case. Without warning, Brianna broke into tears, crying like there was no one in the room with her.

"I can't have the only two people I have left in this world hating each other. Please, I can't take it! I swear I feel like my heart is just going to burst at any moment."

Both Emerson and Jordan said at once, "Stop crying, Brianna."

"Emerson and I will get the funeral together while you go get Roxanne. We will be fine, won't we, Emerson?" Jordan cut her eyes at Emerson and asked.

"Yeah, we will be good," he answered before walking off.

"Thank you so much, Jordan, for everything. I know you swallowing a lot of pride for me right now and I appreciate it." Jordan cracked a smile, "I love you, chic, and that's what sisters are for. You did the same thing for me when I lost Michelle, so it's only right I am here for you when you need me the most."

# 3

The sound of the cool air blowing through the vents was the only sound in the big-body Benz. Emerson was tempted to turn on the music, but he was unsure if Jordan was in the mood or not. He watched her stare out the window for as long as he could before he broke the silence.

"Have you ever planned a funeral before?" Jordan's emerald-bought eyes watered. "No, but I helped out with my sister's funeral," she answered, giving the car window her attention.

"Oh, I'm sorry to hear that."

"It's okay, she's in a better place now. No more worries and no more suffering." Jordan's voice weakened as she pictured her sister, Honey.

"True, I feel bad for poor Skylar. I know she didn't think she was coming up on her last day so quick. You know what I mean?"

"Yeah, I feel you. That's what makes it so sad because she was so young. She left this world at twenty-three years old." Emerson sucked up the disappointment for three long minutes then changed the subject.

"Why are you so mean to me all the time?" Jordan chuckled then replied, "Mean to you?"

"Yeah, mean to me."

Shaking her head side to side, she asked with a beautiful smile gracing her face, " Why do you care?" Emerson giggled for about ten seconds, "Girl you'll a trip." Jordan's warm inviting smile and arrogance was the perfect combination to Emerson.

"What you're going to do when you get a man?"

"I'm going to be me," Jordan quickly replied.

"You're passing the printing place. It's right here to your left." Quickly, Emerson made a U-turn and pulled into The Sam's Printing driveway.

"We're here, Ms. Daisy." The frown on Jordan's face made Emerson laugh yet again.

"I got your Ms. Daisy," Jordan joked.

Well, that's how I feel. I feel like I'm driving Ms. Daisy around," Emerson continued his joking as the two walked into The Sam's Printing. He had been driving Jordan around since morning, getting things together for Skylar's funeral: paying for the funeral, picking out her dress, and finally they were at their last stop for the day, getting Skylar's obituary done.

The night was arriving, and Emerson's stomach was beginning to talk. "Did that noise come from your stomach or your ass?" Jordan asked Emerson with a disturbing look, while he giggled.

"That was my stomach devil in heels. I got to eat, I'm not like you. I don't live off water." For the first time ever, Jordan laughed with Emerson. She knew her image from the outside looked just like Emerson mentioned, a devil in heels plus drinking water all day to stay hydrated didn't help her look at all.

After laughing until she couldn't catch her breath, Jordan said, "I forgot we haven't eaten. Would you like to go eat?" "That would be nice," Emerson answered, rubbing his stomach.

"Let's go to Wet Willy's. I've been having a taste for their wings for a minute now." Jordan left eyebrow raised and her nose tooted.

"Who got money for some Wet Willy's, not me," she snapped.

"As if you have been paying for anything today." Emerson opened the passenger door for Jordan, and she thought, I guess he can be a gentleman when he wants to.

"Let's be clear, you haven't done anything for me. You are paying for your girlfriend's sister's funeral. So, in other words, I'm helping you." Emerson slammed the door on Jordan, and she instantly stops talking. Did he just cut me off with the door? She thought.

"So, Wet Willy's is fine?" He asked, cranking up the Benz.

"Yeah, if you are paying." Ignoring her response, Emerson turned up his radio and the two listened to Jay-z's Black album all the way to Wet Willy's.

"Table for two?" the feminine male waitress asked.

"Yeah," Emerson replied, then the two of them followed the waitress to a booth.

"What can I get you all to drink?"

"I'll have rum on ice."

"And you, ma'am?" The waitress sounded like a proper white woman. "I'll have a coke," Jordan answered with her eyes glued to the menu. "They know they need their asses whooped for these prices. Did you see how much they want for some wings that don't even come with fries?"

"Nah, I usually don't look at the price, and you shouldn't either since you not paying for it." Emerson's arrogance was beginning to resurface, but this time Jordan wasn't disgusted by it.

"Well since you want to be all smart, I'll have some crab legs and wings."

"That's it?" Emerson snickered. "You really don't get out much, do you?" Jordan almost felt embarrassed until she remembered that Emerson wasn't her man or someone, she liked, so it didn't matter what he thought.

"Yes, I get out, I'm just not a thirsty broad who jumps at the opportunity to use a brother." Emerson was impressed and his silence made it clear to Jordan. She took the Coke from the waitress and drank to putting Emerson straight.

"Do we know what we're having?" The waitress whose badge read Trinity asked.

"Yes, I'll have the ten-piece hot wings and the crab legs special."

"Would you like ranch or blue cheese?"

"Blue cheese." Jordan sipped the Coke like it was Hennessy.

"I'll have the same thing but give me a twenty-piece and ranch instead of blue cheese." Emerson took a sip of his rum and then added to his order. "Oh, and a glass of water."

"Coming right up." Trinity twisted off and Emerson began his survey of questions.

"So, where your man at?"

Jordan peeped out the crowd in the restaurant, avoiding eye contact with Emerson.

"He hasn't found me yet."

"That's hard to believe for a woman who seems to have everything in order." Jordan took a deep breath then she replied.

"Well believe it because I'm single and will be until I meet a man on my level." Emerson could feel the frustration coming, but he didn't care. He continued with his survey,

"So, what is your level?"

"A man who knows how to value his woman, care for her and appreciate her presence. You know, the opposite of what you do for Brianna."

Emerson sipped a mouthful of rum, "I care for Brianna just about as much as she cares for herself." Trinity brought over the food and both Jordan and Emerson neglected the conversation. I knew Brianna was the reason for all her men treating her like shit, Jordan thought, while dipping her crispy wet wing into the blue cheese.

"A man treats a woman how a woman treats herself, and I know that's not an excuse to you, maybe, but I'm no fool and I worked hard to get where I'm at in life. If I don't protect myself then nobody will," Emerson rebooted the conversation.

"So, you think Brianna would hurt you, like really Emerson?" Jordan asked between her chews on her wings.

"You say it like it's impossible for me to get hurt. And yeah, I believe Brianna would hurt me if I allowed her to. Brianna is the type of woman that doesn't appreciate a good thing until you show her it's a privilege, if you know what I mean." Jordan choked on her food then smiled. She knew exactly what Emerson meant. She had witnessed Brianna take advantage of some good men, but what was shocking to her was Emerson noticing that Brianna didn't want a good man. That she required a man to treat her like dirt.

"Wow! I plead the fifth on that. Maybe from now on, I'll just stay out of people's business. I just don't like witnessing her getting hurt. I love that girl like a sister, and it hurts me to see her hurt."

"I understand that. That's because you are a good friend. She's lucky to have somebody like you in her life." Jordan and Emerson both sipped their drinks. "Well, if you understand, can you not do what you do or not do it to her when I'm around?"

"Yeah, I got you, little momma." The night had been smoother than Jordan could ever have imagined. Emerson turned out to be everything Jordan couldn't imagine him being and she had finally approved of him and Brianna dating.

# 4

Cars honked their horns as Brianna swerved in and out of lanes. She was driving like a saint out of hell, trying to find peace. Roxanne was killing her nerves and she was beginning to regret the decision to drive back to Atlanta from Alabama. It had only been two days, and Roxanne was already driving Brianna crazy. After hunting for Roxanne for a whole day in every neglected ally, Brianna had to stomach Roxanne blaming her for Skylar's death.

And if that wasn't enough to make Brianna go insane, Roxanne assured Brianna that leaving Jordan with her man was a mistake and took the reward. "Momma, my friends aren't like yours. We don't sleep with each other's men." Roxanne laughed at Brianna then lit her cigarette.

"Girl, you so damn dumb. Jordan is everything you not and that's more of the reason you shouldn't have left her with your man." Brianna stepped on the pedal, trying her best to reach Atlanta before she exploded.

Roxanne continued nagging. "Men get tired of the same thing and as soon as they get the opportunity to smell a new flower, they go for it." The big green veins in Brianna's forehead looked like vicious snakes attacking from the inside. "Roxanne, Jordan and Emerson don't even like each other." Brianna always called Roxanne by her name when she was mad.

"Baby, I'm sorry. I'm not trying to upset you; I just don't want you to get hurt like I did. I was naïve just like you." Skylar and Brianna's father, Lonnie, cheated on Roxanne with her best friend and the two ran off to get married. The pain from the betrayal drove Roxanne into smoking and she never trusted men again. Tears started to decorate Brianna's face and she turned to her mother so that she could see her visible pain.

"What you suppose I did, Momma? Left you in Alabama, buried Skylar without you? You do realize your daughter was just killed, right? All I have heard you talk about is me and Emerson. Forget Emerson for a minute, let's talk about Skylar. All you ever cared about is us having a man and if he was taking care of us."

Brianna always blamed her mother for her bad relationships. She felt her mother raised her girls to be weak, dependable women. She tried for years to be the opposite of her mother, but she failed epically. Every time Brianna looked in the mirror, she saw Roxanne.

She didn't ask for much from men. She took whatever was on the table.

"How dare you question my love for Skylar?" Brianna had hit Roxanne's hot spot and the war began.

"She is my baby girl! I don't want to talk about how I don't have her with me anymore, Brianna. Why would I want to talk about that? Do you know when was the last time I saw my daughter; she was seventeen years old?" Roxanne punched the top of the glove department six times and Brianna silently prayed the airbag wouldn't come out.

"My daughter is gone, and I didn't even get to tell her bye." Brianna secretly wanted to wash her mother's tears away, but her pride stopped her.

"I'll never get to see her pretty face again, hold her close to me, or smell her floral scent." Roxanne had been on drugs for ten years, but she was still intelligent. She drew vivid pictures when she spoke, like some of the best-sellers she wrote.

"I love you, Brianna. That's why I stay on you. I just know how this world can be. You got a good man, and he makes you happy. I don't want you to end up like me: lonely."

Roxanne burst into tears and finally, Brianna swallowed her pride. She rubbed her mother's soft, curly, damaged hair into a ponytail.

"Momma don't cry," she said with static in her voice.

"I didn't mean to hurt you; sometimes I just don't want to hear about boys from you. Sometimes I just want to hear that you love me. But I shouldn't have thrown Skylar in it, that was below the belt. I know you love your daughter, you're her mother. What mother doesn't love her daughter?"

Brianna kissed her mother on the cheek while eyeing the road all at the same time.

"I love you, Brianna, and I'm telling you, you never trust your man and another woman around your man. Don't you be full of trust like I was. I get your point this time, but just keep that in mind for future reference," Roxanne said, chuckling at her joke.

Brianna gripped the steering wheel tight. She couldn't believe that after all she just said to her mother, they ended right back where they started.

Brianna didn't want to think about the negative things Roxanne was suggesting and, she hated her mother for making her life revolve around

her failures. Jordan was like a sister to Brianna and even though Emerson wasn't a saint, his loyalty to Brianna was never questionable.

"Momma, Jordan and Emerson don't even like each other and can barely stay in the same room with one another without exploding." Before Roxanne could even respond, Brianna's negative thoughts did.

The people who hate each other the most are the two people who lust for each other the most.

"Oh right, baby, if you say so." Roxanne's response was dry, and Brianna could feel her negative vibe, so she turned up the radio that was playing low on the gospel channel and sang alone with Kirk Franklin's "Smile."

The ride had been a long one and Brianna was ready to get to her bed. Emerson opened the door and Brianna hugged him tight.

"Damn girl, you act like you have been gone for ages. Come on in so we can shut the door; I got the air on," he said, taking Brianna's arm off around him, then picking up her vintage Channel bag off the floor.

"I know, but it feels like I've been gone for days," Brianna replied, dragging into the house like she had no energy.

"Hey, Roxanne, how are you?" Jordan asked reaching out for a hug. Roxanne's eyes strolled up then down Jordan's body, stopping at her tight pink Victoria's Secret shorts.

"Is that what you walk around in?" Roxanne asked, rejecting Jordan hug. Jordan attempted to cover the length of her shorts with her rejected arms.

"They are not that short, Momma," Jordan laughed, assuming that Roxanne was just being overprotective of her like she used to be back in the day when she and Brianna were growing up.

"I'm not your momma and they are short, short as hell. You don't walk like that around your friend's man." Jordan, Brianna and Emerson all caught the seriousness in Roxanne's voice.

"Oh," Jordan blurted out, stepping back on her left leg with her nose tooted and right brow raised.

"Well, I just put them on if it makes you feel any better. Emerson, can you please take me home because I don't want to be anybody's punching bag. I know everybody is hurting but on the same note everybody is entitled to respect."

"Oh Lord," Brianna murmured, resting her forehead in the palm of her hand, shaking her head side to side.

"Yeah, you might want to leave talking that shit to me you little bitch," Roxanne's tone went from mad to hella mad.

"Please, Emerson, take Jordan home for me, baby." Brianna's head looked as if it would explode if one more word was blurted out by either of the women. Jordan stormed off to the guest room to gather her night bag and on her way out the door she blurted, "I'll be your bitch if you put bad in front of it, bitch!"

# 5

Jordan rocked her seat, shaking her left leg like a loose branch on a tree. "Don't let that damn woman upset you girl." Emerson flashed his pearly white teeth. His smirk made Jordan's smug crack. She joined in on the laughter.

"Don't make me laugh. I'm pissed the fuck off, man." Emerson and Jordan laughed a little more.

"You know Roxanne doesn't have all her damn sense." Slowly, Jordan shook her head no.

"She's no damn fool, she got plenty of sense. What I can't understand is why she would just go off on me like that. I mean, she has never ever spoken to me in that tone and to be honest, it kind of hurt." Emerson's eyes meet Jordan's. "Aww, the baby feelings hurt." Jordan's deep dimples caved, and her eyes sparkled.

"Of course, she never went off on you like that before; you never been stuck in the house with one of Brianna's men with shorts on."

"The shorts weren't even that short and Brianna knows I would never do that to her."

"Brianna don't know that. Why'd you think she didn't come to your rescue?" Jordan continued to shake her head no with her arms resting on her chest. "Brianna's just scary, she plays fence. She never comes to anybody's rescue."

"Brianna didn't take your side because Roxanne was saying what she was thinking. Why you think Brianna never hesitates to put out the house." Emerson's words begin to make sense to Jordan, and she could feel the frustration building.

"Brianna is insecure, and she gets that shit from Roxanne." Jordan was impressed with Emerson. He was no rookie and he had seen right through Brianna. He had seen things that even she was missing.

"I'm just saying don't be no fool and sleep on Brianna. She is no angel. I know she's your friend and everything, but she's got her ways." Jordan tooted her lips, rolled her eyes then added, "You ain't never lied, that's for sure. It's just funny because I always got her back, but she never has mine the same way."

"I always come to her rescue, without a second thought. Shit, I look at the girl like a sister. Especially now, since my sister is dead and gone. But whatever, I'm not even about to burst a blood vessel on Brianna's ass." Emerson changed the mood from frustrated to ease, singing alone with K-Ci & JoJo's *Crazy*.

"Baby you say that you love me, so why are you leaving me." Emerson looked over to Jordan from time to time, singing along with every song until they reached Jordan's place.

"Aye, do you mind if I use your bathroom? I have been holding this shit tomorrow long." Emerson popped off his seat belt as soon as he put the car in park. He didn't wait for Jordan's answer. He grabbed Jordan's

bag for her, "I got it, T, just lead me the way girl." Emerson grabbed a handful of his dick then followed behind Jordan swiftly.

"The bathroom is down the hall on the right," Jordan said as soon as they entered the apartment. "To the right?"

"Yeah, down the hall to the right," Jordan answered before reading the note on the refrigerator that Jasmine left about her being out at her friend's house. Jordan was hoping Jasmine was home, with all the planning for the funeral, she and Jasmine were constantly missing each other.

Jasmine always gave Jordan strength whenever she was feeling down about something. Caring for her niece after her sister had passed gave Jordan a reason to strive for better in life. Since there was no Jasmine, Jordan turned to her Bartenura blue Moscato. Wine was her liquid sleeping pill. Weak from exhaustion, Jordan struggled with getting the bottle open.

"Damn girl you make opening that bottle seem so damn painful." Emerson took the bottle of Moscato from Jordan and popped it right open.

"Oh, this that good shit too." Jordan's dimples marginally deepened. "What you know about this?" she asked, struggling to hide her blushing.

"Man, this is my shit. I like it because it doesn't get me too fucked up." Jordan took two champagne glasses.

"Well, have you a glass then."

"Maybe I will. Do you have some cards around here somewhere?"

"What you need some cards for?" Jordan asked, looking in her kitchen drawer for her playing cards.

"Let's play a hand of something. I'm not in a hurry to get back to that damn house. I need to buy all the time I can." The two burst into laughter, sipping on the Moscato.

"I don't know if that's a good idea. They already think I'm trying to get you. They're definitely going to be thinking something's going on if you show up late."

Emerson made his way to the living area and got good and comfy on the floor, shuffling the cards on the coffee table that was set in the middle of the floor. "That's the difference between me and you. I don't give a rat ass about what people think of me, I'm a grown-ass man and on top of that shit, I pay my own damn bills."

"Well, all right then, boss man," Jordan joked, joining Emerson on the floor. "Quit stalling and let's play some cards." Emerson dealt the first hand.

"I usually don't like playing cards if it's not for money. It's just not fun to me without a gamble." Emerson's smile lit the room.

"Oh, you're a gambler I see. But your money is no good here, I tell you what: if I lose, you win everything in my pocket, if you lose, I get to taste your peaches." Emerson finished the Moscato in his glass and poured him some more.

"What?!" Jordan yelled, choking on her Bartenura. "You heard me."

"I think you did have too much of that Blue over there. Who you think I am?" Emerson ignored Jordan's question and pulled from the deck. "It's your go," he said after dropping the jack of hearts on the table.

"Some people shouldn't drink. It makes them get the cocky disease." Jordan murmured before she dropped her king of clubs.

"And what makes you think I would play second fiddle to anybody else? Then on top of that, you are my best friend's man. Hmm, you done gave me a good laugh for the day." Jordan babbled on and on; she didn't even notice that Emerson had stolen the game right from under her. He took the radio remote off the table and turned-on V-103. The quiet storm soothed the room on low. "You done lost your mind. What do you think you're doing?" Jordan asked after looking at Emerson's winning trunk spread out. Ace of spades and diamond of two.

"I'm about to get what's mine," Emerson answered, then pulled Jordan aggressively towards him.

"No, you are not. Let me go!" Jordan attempted to pull away from Emerson and epically failed. He locked Jordan's legs back with one hand then bent down to her kitty litter and began kissing her through her boy shorts. Her camel toe print hardened his nature instantly.

"Whoever said you had to play second fiddle?" He asked before softly biting on her clit through the shorts. Jordan silently moaned but aggressively lifted Emerson from her peach. "Get up fool, I'm not about to let you taste my shit." The more Jordan fought; the more Emerson craved for her body. He slid her shorts to the side and slid his thumb down her slippery clitoris, digging deep into her hole with his bird finger.

"Aww," Jordan moaned.

"Stop, stop it damnit!" Jordan battled with good and evil. Her body craved Emerson's touch, but her mind despised it. It had been twenty-seven months since she'd had sex, but she had been friends with Brianna over ten years. Jordan's hormones were winning the battle; there was no hope for her morals when Emerson was doing everything so perfect. After surviving scratches and punches to the face and blows to the chest, Emerson ripped Jordan bottoms right off.

"Let me taste this pussy, girl," Emerson blurted out as

he struggled with re-opening Jordan's legs. "Stop fighting it. She's not soaked for decoration." Jordan closed her legs tight once again. "What about Brianna, Emerson? This is not right." Emerson ignored the request for moral respect and finally opened her legs. His tongue vibrated on her clitoris then he slid it right in her hole. His skinny long tongue slid in and out, in and out of her hole.

"Aww Emerson, please." Emerson came up for air with Jordan's juices all over his freshly lined beard. "Please what, Jordan?" Emerson asked, flipping Jordan on her knees, spreading her ass cheek open. "Don't do this."

"It's already done," Emerson responded before he skimmed his tongue down the crack of her ass, massaging her ass cheeks with both of his hands.

"Aww... shit." Jordan began to feel her nut building, so she threw in the white flag and allowed Emerson to collect his pay. R Kelly's '*You Remind Me of Something*' entertained the mood and Jordan let loose. Emerson began to feel Jordan ride his tongue. He knew then Jordan had given in, so he pulled his tongue out her ass and asked, "Do you want me to stop?"

"Aww, no baby, continue."

"What about Brianna?" Emerson teased.

"What about her?" Jordan groaned. "Don't stop until I come all over your face." Emerson smiled at Jordan's demand and continued his quest. He fucked Jordan with his tongue until she drowned him with her juices. Then he squirted his warm semen all over her full breast. When it was all over, Jordan's morals kicked back in, and she threw Emerson out her

house. All his pleading to lay with her up to sunrise didn't work. She was disgusted with her decision and didn't want to be reminded of it every time she looked into his manipulative eyes.

# 6

The grieving audience watched Jordan closely, patiently waiting for her to share her memories of Skylar.

"I remember when I lost my older sister, Michelle, and I felt like the world had come tumbling down on my head. I felt like I had no one. My mother was gone, my father was a disappearing act, and now I had no sister." Jordan sniffled and struggled to get her words out. She wiped her running nose with the Kleenex the usher had given her.

"Skylar held me close and so tight I couldn't feel my pain anymore. It was like she took the pain for me." The tears Jordan tried to hold back poured down her round cheeks.

"I say that to say, I lost yet another sister. I love you, baby girl, and I pray that your beautiful soul rests in peace."

Brianna's weeping grew louder; she could barely catch her breath. The usher rushed to the front row to give her and Roxanne more Kleenex.

The elderly lady from the old Joyland community got up to sing the same song she sung at every member of Joyland's funeral, Catch on Fire.

"Oh, I wish somebody here would catch on fire." Before she could get the fire out good, the room of grieving people broke into tears. You could

hear Roxanne, Brianna and Jordan's voices over everybody else. The family followed close behind Skylar's casket, crying until she was locked away in the funeral car.

"Where is Roxanne?" Jordan asked, struggling, trying to pick Brianna up off the floor.

"She's probably in somebody's alley. You know she couldn't take this." Brianna's voice was hoarse, and her mascara was running all over the place.

"Come on, let me get you to the bed. You need some rest, Brianna." Jordan toted Brianna to her bed and tucked her in then turned on the ceiling fan.

"Jordan, where are you going?" Brianna whined.

"I'm going to get you something to help you sleep."

"Okay, has Emerson made it back yet?" Brianna struggled with getting her words out. She couldn't stop crying. Her heart felt as if it was ripped out of her chest.

"I don't think so, but I'll check. Stop crying, Brianna, you are breaking my heart baby." Jordan whined. "I'll see if he's back, just lay down."

"He's probably out with some bitch when I need him most," Brianna blurted before tucking her head under her pillow. Jordan shook her head no in disgust.

"Just relax, he'll be back. He knows you need him." The lie began ripping right through Jordan's heart. She couldn't believe how she had betrayed her best friend, especially when Brianna needed her now more than ever. She cursed herself out while pouring Brianna up some Bartenura Blue Moscato, "You know better than this shit, Jordan. How could you?" Tears rolled down Jordan's rosy cheeks.

"God, please forgive me. I know I was wrong, and I ask that you please forgive me for my wrong-doing."

Jordan's legs began to shake. She felt like they were going to give out on her, so she bent down on her knees and continued her prayer. "God, please give Brianna the strength she needs to stay through her time of need; Lord, please touch her aching soul." Jordan broke down; she could no longer hold in her cries. She sobbed so loud she had to put her hands over her mouth so Brianna couldn't hear her.

"Pull it together, Jordan. Brianna needs you," she whispered to herself before pulling herself up on the counter to get the glass of Moscato.

"Here, Brianna, take this. Drink it down with this." Brianna looked at the sleeping pill, then quickly swallowed it down with the Moscato. "Thank you, friend, for being here. I know it's been hard on you too." Jordan rubbed her fingers through Brianna's long black hair.

"You don't have to thank me, Brianna, that's what friends are for." Jordan pressed her lilac-soft lips against Brianna's chocolate cheeks. "I love you sister." Jordan's glossy lips wiped up Brianna's left puddle of tears.

"I love you too, you cow." The two did what was hard to do, they laughed. After twenty minutes Brianna was fast asleep.

"Wake up, beautiful." Jordan's body turned from one side to another. "Wake up sleepyhead," Emerson whispered into Jordan's ears.

"What are you doing here?" Jordan asked after blinking her eyes twice. "I want you, Jordan. I want you all to myself." Emerson's full lips drowned Jordan's neck with kisses. "Stop, boy, are you crazy?! Brianna is in the next room." He ignored Jordan and continued to trail her body with his warm kisses.

"So what? She's asleep."

Jordan lifted Emerson's heavy head off her neck, "Stop, damn it! I'm not playing with you. I can't do this anymore. It's not right, I can't do this to Brianna. She is like my sister and my soul just can't rest at night with that kind of betrayal on my chest." Emerson flung Jordan's thick sunrise-gold hair off her shoulders and began to trace moist kisses on her shoulders then down to her nipple piercing. "It's too late for that shit now. I want you and I'm going to have you."

He pulled her body in toward him by her waist.

"Either you throw in the white flag, or I go wake her up now and let her know what the deal is." Jordan couldn't believe her ears. It was very clear that she was in way too deep to back out now. As she stared at the ceiling, tears begin to roll down her face, resting on her neck.

"Aww," she whispered, trying not to wake up Brianna. "Emerson, go deeper, baby, please." She dug his face in deeper and he ate it like it was his last supper.

"Jordan, I want you on my arm, baby. Brianna not the girl for me," he said, wiping off Jordan's juices while gliding his hard steel up and down her clitoris.

"Say you want this shit, Jordan." The sound of his balls slapping against her wet hole sounded off.

"I want this shit, Emerson, I want it," she replied with tears dripping from her face. Jordan was sprung out on lust, and she needed rehab. Emerson's sex was like a toxic drug and his cockiness was her cigarette. Jordan felt for Emerson's touch.

"Damn, this pussy hungry for this dick, baby." He whispered into her ears while slowly pounding her cherry.

"Tell me you're mine, Jordan. Tell me I'm not dreaming."

"Aww, you not dreaming, Emerson. I'm yours baby; I can't fight it anymore. You win, baby, now beat me." Everything Jordan stood for went right out the door and all six inches of Emerson's hard dick plunged into Jordan's gut. She scratched the back of his neck then his waves, holding on tight to his muscular physique, enjoying his every stroke.

"I'm coming, baby, I'm coming." Emerson beat the cat harder, "Come on then, wet this dick up." Jordan placed the pillow over her mouth. She couldn't risk Brianna hearing her scream Emerson's name.

"Aww, Emerson, baby, that shit feels good." After three more strokes Emerson released his babies into Jordan's guts.

"Fuck, I hope we conceived my son," he said before he flopped down to the right side of the bed. "It's official, you mine." Emerson's teeth gripped Jordan's ear lobe, then he slid his tongue down her sweaty neck, ending his mission with a soft kiss.

"Treat yourself tomorrow. You've been everybody shoulder to cry on. You need a break." Emerson picked up his slacks off the floor and tossed a stack of hundreds in Jordan's knockoff Michael Kors bag.

"Now it's time you had somebody to lean on." He said before he exited the room.

# 7

---

Brianna walked into the Chanel store, looking fine to the nines, flaunting her stuff as if she owned the boutique.

"Hello, how are you?" the beautiful sales associate asked the girls as they made their way into the high fashion boutique.

"We're fine, and how are you today?" Jordan responded.

"Oh, I'm great," the sale associate smoothly ended her assistance of her current customer so she could assist Brianna. Brianna was a regular and the S.A. knew Brianna spent good money, and big sales meant good commissions for her.

"What can I get for you today, Ms. Brianna?" the associate asked with her perky spirit.

"I came in for one thing today, Vanessa, so I'm going to need you to help me do just that."

Jordan flashed a smirk then added, "You sound like a damn addict, girl." The girls all laughed.

"I believe I am, girl, but I'll get help another day. Today, I need a little shopping therapy." Brianna picked through the beautiful blouses on the rack.

"So, what was the main item you came in for, so I can grab it for you?" Tiffany the associate asked, flashing her pearly white teeth.

"I'd like to get the lady T bag." Brianna said.

"Oh okay, you're right on time because we only have two of them left." Tiffany walked over to the shelf and grabbed the gorgeous red jumbo classic flap bag. "Will this be all for you?" Brianna glanced over at Jordan.

"You want something, girl? It's on me." Jordan stood with her arms resting on her breast, shaking her head no.

"You sure?" Brianna asked again.

"Yeah, I'm sure girl. I'm good. You know, I don't believe in spending this kind of money for no reason." Tiffany took one look at Jordan's Old Navy romper and thong sandals and knew she wasn't telling a lie about her budget.

"I forgot how cheap your butt is." With no shame Jordan smiled and said, "Hell yeah, I don't play that. Shit, I have a mouth to feed." Brianna searched inside her Chanel clutch for her credit card.

"That will be $536.52." Brianna gave her card to the cashier then resumed her conversation.

"Speaking of an extra mouth to feed, how is Ms.

Jasmine?" Before Jordan could answer Brianna, the cashier interrupted.

"I'm sorry ma'am, this card has been declined."

"What?" Brianna looked at the cashier as if she was speaking Spanish.

"Oh, try it again, Vanessa, she's a regular," Tiffany said to the cashier. Without a problem and with a smile on her face, Vanessa swiped the card once more.

"It's still reading declined, I'm sorry." Tiffany took the card from Vanessa and tried it once more.

"I'm sorry, do you have another, Ms. Brianna?" Jordan could see Brianna's blood boiling. Her thick green veins made their way to her forehead.

"Well can I get it?" The customer Tiffany once abandoned for Brianna asked.

"What the fuck you mean, can you get it?" Brianna snapped. "It must be something wrong with yawl machine or something because it's nothing wrong with my card. All of my credit card bills are up to date and paid for." Vanessa, Tiffany, and the waiting customer all looked at Brianna sideways. Brianna couldn't believe the cold treatment, she had spent good money with this Chanel boutique, she didn't get the memo that it was strictly business and always, always about the dollar. No one was your friend; they were only friendly to the dollar bill.

"I got it. It's fine." Jordan reached into her purse and peeled off five hundred and fifty dollars in cash. "You don't have to; I don't need to give these motherfuckers any more of my money anyway." Brianna's voice carried throughout the store, and of course, they had all eyes on them. Tiffany took the money from Jordan's hands, completely shocked that she even had that type of cash on her.

"Thank you for your services," Tiffany said to the girls as she gave Jordan her change.

"Girl, let's go; I don't have time for this fake bullshit." Jordan followed Brianna out of the boutique.

"What's up Brianna? How are you holding up?" Fat Boy, Emerson's best friend, spotted Brianna coming out of the store and approached her.

"Oh, I'm trying to stay strong, Fat Boy. How are you?" Brianna responded, resting her arm on her large black Chanel shopping bag.

"That's good, ma, I hate that shit happened to Skylar man, I couldn't believe that shit when Emerson told me." "Yeah, I know," she responded dryly.

Fat Boy noticed Brianna's eyes were getting watery, so he changed the subject quick. "Who is this you got with you?" He asked, looking Jordan up and down.

"Oh, this is my best friend, Fat Boy. Yawl never met before?"

"Nah, I never met her. I think I would've remembered meeting a sexy thing like mama." Fat Boy's accent made it no secret that he was from New York.

"We met before, you just never looked me in my face.

Your eyes were fixated on my ass." Fat Boy burst into laughter, rubbing his round stomach.

"Oh, you are feisty, I see, but you can't blame a man ma. Look at you, with your sexy ass." Jordan cracked a crooked smile and shook her head no. She wasn't at all turned on or interested.

"Well, you should probably try and approach her the right way, Fat Boy. I mean, she is single, smart, and got her own." Jordan cut her eyes at Brianna.

*Oh, I can't even believe she went there, I'm going to kill Brianna's ass,* Jordan thought to herself but didn't take away her crooked smile. She continued to stare him down like he was the scum beneath the earth.

"Nah, she not ready for a real nigga man," he responded, scratching his swollen round head that set under a New York baseball cap.

"Nah, she not ready Fat Boy." Brianna took a good look at Jordan and saw she wasn't having it.

"You got my number if she changes her mind," Fat Boy said after he kissed Brianna on the forehead.

"Keep your head up baby-girl."

"I will; I'll keep in touch with you." Fat Boy cracked a smile and walked away.

"You do that," he said before he was completely out of the girls' range.

"Girl, why are you looking like that?" Jordan's nose was tooted as if she smelled the worst shit in her life. "Fat Boy got that money, why're you playing?"

"Girl, I don't give a damn about no money; he is not my type." Brianna burst into laughter, "You're crazy and picky as shit. But I guess you couldn't care about him having money, shit you walk around with motherfucking whoops in your purse like a dope boy." Jordan continued to shake her head. "Thank you though for the bag; I don't know why my shit declined."

"You good, I know how your ass is about these damn materials. I just want you to take your mind off your pain, and if shopping does the trick for you, then so be it." Brianna almost wanted to cry, but she tried her hardest to keep her tears tucked away.

"Thank you for being such a great friend, Jordan. I'm telling you, I wouldn't know what the fuck to do if you weren't here by my side, man, for real." The hood slang Brianna tried hard to hide around Emerson slowly resurfaced.

"You know I got you bitch, now come on; let's go. I got to go to Jasmine's basketball game. She cheers tonight."

"Aww, she is a cheerleader. I can't wait to see her in her uniform."

# 8

---

The smell of cheap hot dogs boiling, and buttery popcorn perfumed the crowded gym.

"Girl, you know I got to get me some nachos and one of them damn hot dogs," Brianna said to Jordan.

"I know, girl. Don't this just bring back memories?" Jordan and Brianna made their way through the crowd, to the concession stand.

"Yes girl, I miss my high school days," Brianna responded.

"Hey Jasmine's momma!" Jordan flaunted her beautiful smile and ignored correcting Jasmine's friend's confusion.

"Hey, Shakira, how much are those hot dogs, honey?"

"It depends on what you want on them." Shakira slid Jordan the hand-written menu with the list of foods and prices.

"Oh okay, give me the nachos fully loaded and,"

Jordan turned to Brianna before ending her order and asked, "What you are getting?" Before Brianna could answer Jordan's first question, she threw another one. "Do you want to share a hot dog with me, and I share my nachos with you?"

"Yeah, we can do that because I don't need to be eating all that shit by myself. I'll be in the bathroom all night." The girls burst into laughter.

"What would you like on that hot dog?" Shakira asked Brianna.

"Um, you can put some chili, slaw, and onions, oh and a little of that nacho cheese too." The girls' food was ready in less than three minutes. They took their food and found them a seat in the bleachers close to the cheering squad.

"Swoosh that ball, put in for two, we're the mighty Tigers and we do not lose," Jordan and Brianna chanted along with their old cheer with Jasmine. And when it came time for Jasmine to do her toe, Jordan screamed out loud, "Show them how it's done, baby!" Jordan's motherly ways tickled Brianna.

"Girl, you sound like an old damn lady. Sit down."

"Shit, I don't care. That's my damn baby and she be killing them damn jumps, girl. Did you see how far up she can go?" Brianna took another look at the girls who were still taking turns showing off their jumps.

"Yeah, she did jump higher than everybody."

"That's what I'm saying! She better than all of them damn girls on that damn team, but they didn't give her the captain position." The mothers behind Jordan looked at her sideways, but they didn't bother saying anything. They noticed that Jordan was much younger and clearly had a lot to learn about respect and parenting.

"Well, you know how that is sometimes, mother fuckers were haters then. I'm sure there are some haters now." Even though Brianna secretly felt like Jasmine wasn't better than the captain, she didn't exclaim that to her friend. She was itching to be down with Jordan wanted to be down

with Jordan since it had been a minute since she was all up in that scene. Emerson had been the only team she cheered for in a long time.

"Yeah, that's why I always let her know, no matter what, keep doing you because you are going to have haters. You're young, beautiful, and smart. The haters are bound to hate." Brianna hated how Jordan paraded Jasmine on a higher pedestal than others, but she kept quiet and didn't give her opinion. But the truth of the matter was that Jasmine wasn't a saint, and the entire neighborhood was aware of her scheming and tricks. The only person who was in the blinds about the known facts was Jordan. Tired of hearing about Jasmine, Brianna changed the subject.

"Girl, who is that?" Brianna asked Jordan pointing at the basketball coach.

"Oh, that's the basketball coach," Jordan responded.

"Girl, you need to follow him right out of this gym."

Brianna's green-bought eyes followed the coach's tight ass out the gym.

"Girl, I'm not trying to talk to no damn school coach." Jordan tooted her nose and rolled her eyes like Brianna had just suggested the worst hook-up ever.

"Girl, you are too damn picky. Who the hell you think gone come and save your ass?" Brianna stayed on a mission to get Jordan a man. She felt that if Jordan had a man, she wouldn't be so uptight and judgmental when it came to life.

"I don't need no man. Hell, when the right man comes, he'll come." Brianna rolled her eyes once more then blurted, "That's bullshit!" The parents behind Jordan and Brianna chimed in uninvited with laughter. Jordan's answer just wasn't persuasive; no one bought it.

"Jasmineyyy!" Brianna waved her hand for Jasmine to come to her. "Why are you calling her out of line, Brianna? She's not supposed to move." Brianna ignored Jordan and continued to wave Jasmine to her.

"Come here for a second, baby." Jasmine's healthy honey-blonde wrap bounced as she skipped over to the bleachers like a kid.

"Do you know if your coach has a wife?" Brianna whispered into Jasmine's ear.

"You can't whisper, bitch, and don't be asking her nothing like that, girl, that's her damn coach." Brianna waved Jordan off and continued to whisper into

Jasmine's ear. Jasmine giggled; she was down on the scheme. No one wanted Jordan to have a man more than Jasmine.

"Don't worry. I got it; I know what to say. I'm going to hook it up." I bet you do know what to say with your grown-ass, Brianna thought to herself.

"Hook what up?" Jasmine, don't you go asking that damn man nothing crazy, girl; I'm not playing. Jasmine ignored Jordan and skipped right out the game and to the concession stand where the coach was ordering a Powerade.

Jordan bowed her head the moment she saw the coach take out his phone and begin dialing numbers. Brianna giggled like she was one of the high school kids. "Oops, I guess he is available." Jordan shook her head no in shame. "Look up Jordan," Brianna said. Jordan decided to take the mature route out and held her head high. Jasmine pointed her out to the coach, and he nodded his head at Jordan.

"Girl, I got a feeling you gon thank me for this later."

Jordan tried her best not to laugh since the coach was still watching so she murmured, "I'm going to kill you bitch."

"Come on, let's go before this crowd starts leaving," Brianna said, leading Jordan out the door and right into the coach.

"Why you didn't come over here yourself, girl? You're gonna have people thinking I'm talking to your daughter?" The coach and Jasmine stood in front of the exit door.

"Oh, Jasmine is her niece, not her daughter," Brianna cleared the air. She didn't want any stop signs to interfere with this hook-up.

"Oh, you not Jasmine's mother?" The coach's shocked face expression made it clear that he was confused with this new information.

"No, she's, my niece. She moved in with me after my sister died." His confusion was clear now. He nodded his head yes, rubbing his neatly cut Rick Ross beard.

"Oh okay, I know I see you up at the school a lot."

"Yeah, I'm up here a lot checking up on her butt, making sure she's doing what she's supposed to do." Jasmine curled up like a baby under Jordan and said, "I'm always good," in her sweetest voice.

"Yeah, she okay. I don't know about always good," he said. "But it is okay to call you, right?" the coach waved his iPhone and asked.

"Yeah, it's okay; you can do that. My name is Jordan." Brianna smiled and gave Jasmine the "you go girl look."

"Okay Jordan, I'm Coach Robertson."

Jordan couldn't understand for the life of her why she wasn't interested in Coach Robertson since he was everything she had been

asking for in a man; fine, young, employed, and respectful. Confused, she secretly prayed Emerson had nothing to do with her lack of interest.

# 9

---

The hard-brown cognac swirled around the ice cubes as Emerson wobbled his glass. He had been watching the door for hours, and finally, after three hours, the doorknob slowly turned. He picked up the nine and cocked it back, pointing it towards the door.

"What the hell are you doing?" Brianna nearly jumped out of her skin at the sight of Emerson's pistol. "Girl I just like to blow your fucking head off." She passed her right hand over her chest and took a deep breath. "You scared me half todeath. And why are you sitting in here drinking with the lights off?" Brianna's eye's followed Emerson's eyes to the clock mounted on the wall.

"It's fucking 2:13 in the morning. Where the fuck have you been?" Emerson could hear Brianna swallow her saliva; she was sweating bricks, and her eyes were bulging wide.

"I went to the game with Jordan to see her little

niece cheer, then we ended up going to the Waffle House after and we talked about so much, I lost track of time." Brianna's weak voice and obedience were like an invitation for Emerson to knock her the hell out. He truly believed that Brianna secretly desired to be hit, and most times he would grant her wish, but this time he just paraded his strength in her

~ 54 ~

face. He bucked up at Brianna as if he was going to dot her eye, and she flinched just like he knew she would.

"I should punch you dead in your mother fucking eye for that bullshit ass lie. I know your ass been out there whoring." Emerson knew in his heart that Brianna wasn't cheating, but he wanted her to be so he pretended she was so he could have a reason to be free.

"I wasn't with no nigga, Emerson, you can call Jordan and ask her." Brianna's speech was no longer hood-slang, but one of a proper girl.

"Yeah, like that bitch gone tell me the truth."

"I'm not lying to you, I swear, Emerson." Brianna covered her face as Emerson circled her.

"I'm so sick of your shit. You come in here late in the fucking morning like I don't have to get up in the morning. Then I try to comfort you in your time of need, and you'd rather go out and let a bitch on the street have your time if that's even true." Emerson stormed out the seating area and upstairs to the master bedroom.

"I'm tired of trying to show you how to be the woman for me, Brianna. I'm through with this fucking joke of a damn relationship." Emerson picked up his bag that was pre-packed, sitting by the door. "You can have the condominium, it's paid for." Tears begin to shower from Brianna's eyes. "What are you talking about, Emerson? What are you doing?" Brianna smacked Emerson's bag to the floor.

"I'm leaving you, Brianna... it's over. I can't do this anymore." Brianna broke down sobbing. She felt like she was at yet another funeral.

"Don't do this shit to me, Emerson. You're all I have baby. I can't lose you too." Brianna broke down to her knees with her hands pasted to her face while she cried her heart out.

"Stop crying, Brianna, you had to know this was coming. We haven't been happy for a long time now, and personally, I'd just rather be alone than to be with someone and not be happy." Brianna's sobbing increased.

"I can make you happy, just give me a chance. I know I haven't been myself, but I just lost my sister, damnit!" she said, holding her stomach. The betrayal was hurting her worse than a pregnant woman with contractions.

"We were unhappy way before your sister's death, Brianna. Come on, you know that." Emerson was no longer the monster he had prepped all that night to be. He wanted badly to comfort Brianna, but he knew that wasn't the best move at the moment, so he went to plan B and dropped twenty grand on the nightstand.

"Here is a little something for you until you can find you a job."

Brianna looked at the money on the stand and said, "I can't believe you are doing this to me, Emerson, after all we been through."

"Don't make this harder than it has to be, Brianna. I will always care for you, you know that. And if you ever need me, I'm here, but I'm just in a place in my life where I don't need a girl."

Brianna jumped to her feet and slammed her fist into Emerson's hard chest. "If I need you, you'll be here?" She repeated his words back to him, hoping he would get how silly it sounded. "I need you now, Emerson, I need you now more than ever and you turning your back on me. How fucking dare, you, asshole!" Emerson covered his face and Brianna pounded right into his forearm.

"Quit, girl, before you hurt yourself," he said as Brianna shook off the pain from hitting him. "This the shit I'm talking about right here; you don't know how to act."

"How the hell you expect me to act when my man tells me he's leaving me right after burying my sister?" she snapped.

"Like you got some damn sense, that's how," he responded.

"Look, I got to go. I need some air and some time to clear my mind; this shit got me bugging." Brianna stood in front of the door with her legs and arms stretched out.

"Look move, Brianna! I don't have time for this shit; I need to go." Emerson lifted Brianna up off her feet and moved her to the side, "I'll be back for my things. Get you some rest, man."

Brianna began beating Emerson on his back as he walked to the front door. "Don't do this shit to me, Emerson. I love you! I don't want anybody else but you, I swear." Emerson ignored Brianna's cry and began walking even faster out down the stairs.

"What do you want from me?" She yelled to his back. "I've given you all of me and this is how you repay me?"

Finally, Emerson was at the door. "Keep it together, Brianna. You have your whole life ahead of you," he said before slamming the door behind him.

"Why me, Lord?" she cried out with her back against the door. "Why take everything I love away from me? What have I done? Please tell me, so I don't do it again, please, Lord." Her sobbing was so intense she could barely breathe. She took long pauses between cries. "I--------give---myself to---you Lord," sniffing, "Please—help me, God."

The intense commotion between Emerson and Brianna had him bugging. Brianna was on repeat in his mind, "How could you leave me when I need you most?" It was all he could hear playing in his head. He tried turning up the quiet storm on v-103, but nothing was doing it. No music could drown his guilt.

# 10

---

**B**ath and Body Work tropical island candles and lemon pine soul both perfumed throughout Jordan's apartment. With a little help from Jodeci, she could clean every inch of the apartment within hours. It was only once a blue moon when Jordan could have the apartment to herself. With Jasmine gone over her friend's house for the weekend, she could get in some cleaning and have a little downtime for herself.

Boom, boom, boom; the knocks at the door startled Jordan. She rewrapped her toweled breasts tighter then peeked out the peephole before saying, "Who is it?"

"It's me, Jordan. Can I talk to you?" Emerson fidgeted like a young boy in trouble with his mother. He didn't know what to expect from Jordan. He knew she wasn't the type of girl to accept an uninvited visit.

"Shit! What the fuck is he doing here?" Jordan muttered. She rewrapped the towel around her once more then opened the door. "What are you doing here?" she asked as soon as she opened the door.

"I can't do it no more. I'm done with that bitch, I'm through!" Emerson invited himself in. He began to pace her floor back and forth trying to draw up emotions; so Jordan wouldn't grill him for popping up at her home uninvited.

"You through with what? What's going on now?" Jordan peeked her head out the door to check if anyone had seen Emerson come in, then she quickly closed the door behind him.

"I can't deal with that girl. She is too dramatic for me." Emerson stopped pacing the floor then eyed Jordan standing in her white towel. "You want the truth?" he asked in a calmer tone. "Please and thank you," she responded.

"You the only one here?" he asked, attempting to change the subject. The hard air Jordan released from her mouth was evidence to Emerson that she was growing irritated; he had to get it together quick. So, he walked over to Jordan and wrapped his arms around her waist.

"I just want you," he whispered. She shook her head no and he whispered, "Why not? I know you want me too because I wouldn't be here if you didn't." Emerson softly kissed Jordan on her neck.

"You wouldn't allow me this close to you if you weren't feeling the same thing I'm feeling." Jordan could feel his manhood rising as he held her close. "Give us a chance, Jordan." Emerson's hands slowly roamed to her soft round ass.

"It will never work Emerson; you belong to Brianna."

"You're the only person I'm trying to belong to, Jordan." Deep down she knew the words Emerson was saying could very much be plotted in his blueprint to get to her cookies, but she couldn't see past what she wanted: an opportunity to have a happy ever after. She took a step back from Emerson.

"Please, baby, don't deny us a fair chance because of her. If she is really your friend, she'll understand." Jordan ignored Emerson's plea and dropped her towel.

They looked at each other with desire even though they both knew they had no business being together like that. In the heat, he said, "Let me help."

She could manage nothing but "Okay." He lifted her left leg up on the end of the coach then shoved three of his fingers into her dripping vagina. "Aww!" she moaned. The initial thrust felt great. He fucked her with his three fingers. The experience was so intense, she began to pinch her nipples.

And with both hands available at the time, she pushed her breasts together and pushed them up towards her mouth, licking on her own nipples. He noticed she was about to explode, so he took his fingers out her kitty and said, "No, I don't want you to cum yet!" He put his fingers up to her mouth then said, "Lick it! Taste yourself for me." As he held his fingers in place, she placed her hand over his and began to lick her pussy juice clean. As soon as she finished, he gave her a kiss.

He sucked on her bottom lip, withdrawing a quick sample of her nectar from it. Emerson slowly put his fingers back into Jordan's swollen pussy and began to finger fuck her once again. But this time, he sucked on her breasts.

Jordan cupped her left titty in her hand and fed it to him. He was grateful to have it. After a few moments, she fed him the other one too. He pulled her hips upwards a little more towards him so that her ass was exposed just enough for him to finger it to. She couldn't hold back anymore. She came harder than she had ever cum before and judging from his reaction, she assumed he came as well even though his dick never left his pants. He pulled his cum-drenched fingers out from her pussy and devoured every drop of it.

"I hope you don't think that's it?" he asked, flaunting his beautiful smile.

"Nah, I know that's not it." Emerson began to tremble as Jordan went down on her knees, unbuckling his belt on her way down.

"Well, I guess it's time I marked my territory," she said while working on getting his dick out of his pants. "Do you mind if I mark my territory?"

Emerson was speechless; she hungrily took in the head of his penis, letting her tongue slide in and out of the slit. Some of his juices immediately started to escape. "Oh, damn," he whispered,

"Um, yes, baby," she responded before she went for the trophy. For the next thirty minutes, she sucked on him like he was royalty.

He came the first time in less than five minutes, but Jordan wouldn't let it go at that. She intended to teach him how to last longer by doing great head. She could tell he wasn't used to his dick being sucked so good, so she took advantage of his weakness. After she deep throated his Mandingo until he came in her mouth three times, she glanced at the grandfather clock in the entry hall and noticed it was three o'clock. "Oh, we are going all night baby." She whispered.

Jordan walked over to the front of the sofa and spread her legs. "Come eat me."

Emerson didn't know how to act. He wasn't used to being bossed around. He usually did all the shot calling. Like a fat kid with cake, Emerson ate on Jordan's pussy until it was swollen.

It was obvious that eating pussy was something he didn't need schooling on. By the time he finished eating on Jordan's cookie, he was ready to blow once more. He quickly shoved his dick into Jordan pussy and muttered, "Your pussy about to swallow these babies. Fuck that!" Jordan gripped on tight to Emerson's back with one hand and pushed

down on his tight ass with the other so that his dick would shove deeper into her pussy.

"Yes baby, get all of it in me," she moaned.

"Aww, bitch, this pussy's good... fuck---!" he screamed as his ass tightened and his soldiers released.

For at least ten minutes after that great nut, they were speechless. They cuddled up on the sofa recovering from what had just taken place. Emerson stared at Jordan while he ran his hand across her shaved-naked pussy. They lay, still basking in the afterglow, the only sounds in the room the rotating blades of the box fan.

"This was the best fucking night of my life." Emerson broke the silence then thrust his tongue down Jordan's throat. "You done fucked up now and you don't even know it."

Jordan grinned at Emerson and the two began to tongue wrestle some more and all night until they were both fast asleep in each other's arms.

# 11

---

Jordan slowly pulled the seven-fifty up to the curb. The beautiful cozy bungalow home had her speechless. Her mouth hung open and her eyes fixated on the breathtaking home. "I take it this is your type of home right here?" Emerson watched Jordan out of the corner of his eyes with a warm smile.

"Yes, I love it." Jordan didn't waste any more time. She put the car in park and jumped out to greet the realtor.

"Welcome to Brookhaven, Atlanta's newest city!" Janice the realtor greeted Emerson and Jordan with a large welcoming smile. "Did you have trouble finding the home?"

"No, not at all. I remember driving through this neighborhood before it was developed." Jordan responded.

"Well come on, let me show you the home." Emerson and Jordan followed Janice into the home.

"Oh wow! I love this open concept." Jordan slipped out her red Kardashian collection pumps and set them by the door.

"What you think so far, Mr. Waters?"

Emerson walked over to the gas stove and said, "So far so good. I see you got one of the most important things off my wish list."

Janice smiled and reached from one ear to another, "I told you, you were going to love this home."

The blonde tucked her wrap behind her ear then asked, "Is this home for the both of you or are you just assisting Mr. Waters today?" Before Jordan could answer Janice, Emerson chimed in.

"I'm hoping it's for the both of us." He pressed his steel against Jordan's soft bottom then wrapped his hands around her thin waist. "So that means you must knock her off her feet with this house, Janice."

"Oh, I'm sure that won't be hard to do," the realtor joked, and Jordan cut her eyes at Emerson. His charming ways had her feeling some type of way.

Janice glided her hands across the beautiful granite. "Do you like the countertops?"

"Yes, I love them. I love the stainless steel as well." Jordan opened the dark cabinets. "I see the cabinets are new as well."

"Yes, everything has been updated. Let's go see the upstairs. I have a surprise for you, something I know you will love."

Emerson followed behind the women slowly. Tired of Brianna calling, he finally answered, "What do you want?" he asked aggressively.

"Where are you? We need to talk." Emerson released hot, hard air. Frustrated, he snapped.

"We don't have anything to talk about Brianna, nothing!"

"Why are you fucking whispering? You around a bitch or something?" Brianna asked.

"No, I'm trying to find me somewhere to stay and I don't have time to do this shit with you?" Janice and Jordan watched silently as Emerson bickered back and forth with Brianna. "Listen, man, if you call me one more time, I'm going to block your damn number."

Emerson ended the call and joined the girls in the Master bedroom. "Now, what did I miss?" he joked.

"Well, I was just about to show Ms. Jordan the closet of paradise."

Janice opened the walk-in closet, and sure enough, the closet was paradise. The closet was big enough to be another room, but Jordan didn't seem interested anymore. Her heart melted when Emerson ended the call with Brianna so hostilely; her guilt was loud, and Emerson could hear it. He walked over to her and whispered in her ear, "I had to be aggressive because if I hadn't, she'll think I'm not mad with her and I just don't want to lead her on because that will just hurt her more." The Caucasian realtor didn't know what to do. The energy in the room began to become awkward.

"Janice, we'll take the house; you can get the paperwork started." Jordan walked out of the room in silence and Janice stood still with confusion.

"Did you want to see the other homes I had for you?" Janice asked Emerson with a plastered smile.

"No, this one will do. She loves this one."

"Okay, well I'll give you a call once I hear from the owners." Emerson quickly paced out the door behind Jordan.

"What's up? Talk to me." Emerson slammed the car door destructively.

"I just feel like shit right now!" Jordan rested her head on the steering wheel as tears slowly leaked from her eyes. "I'm torn, Emerson. I like you but I love Brianna. She's my best friend and you don't treat people you love this way." Jordan began sobbing.

"Don't cry Jordan." Emerson softly kissed her on the forehead, "You want me to drive?" he asked.

"No, I'm good." Jordan put the car in drive and the two rode in silence all the way to Jordan's house.

"Hello, welcome to Buck Head Pawning," the Caucasian greeted Brianna with her cheery spirit as soon as Brianna opened the door.

"Oh, I'm doing fine." Brianna opened her Chanel bag and threw all of Emerson's jewelry on top of the counter. "What can you give me for this? And don't bullshit me; I know how much it's worth." The sales associate gawked at the jewelry like a dog on red meat.

"Okay, let me get my supervisor for you." Brianna waited ten long minutes for the supervisor.

"Hey, how are you ma'am?"

"I'm fine, but I'll be even better if you are coming out here with the right number." Brianna flaunted her beautiful smile.

"Well, that's what I'm here for: to make your day better than yesterday," he responded with a deep-south country accent. He and Brianna laughed at his response for a quick second before they jumped right into business. "So, I'm sure you know I can't give you what you paid for this pile of Jordans?"

Brianna raised her left eyebrow. "Yeah, I'm aware of that, but what number did you have in mind?"

Fat Boy bit down his lips, staring at the pile, hoping he wouldn't blurt out the wrong number. "I can give you fifteen thousand."

"$15,500 and we got a deal," Brianna responded with a non-negotiable scowl on her face.

"You got it," the white man racked up the jewelry. "Get this woman her money, Cheryl," he said to the sales associate.

Brianna pocketed her check and strutted out the pawnshop like Bernadine did after she burned John's clothes and car up. Brianna felt in control. She had already sold all of Emerson's clothes to the hood boys who worshiped designer clothes and shoes. She had even taken Emerson's Benz to the chop shop to have the serial numbers removed and color changed from black to white, then she reported it stolen.

Brianna wanted to hit Emerson where it hurt, but she wanted to make sure she benefited in the process. There was no way he was just going to leave her dead and dry.

# 12

The vibrating phone slid across the nightstand. It was only an inch away from falling onto the floor before Jordan caught it.

"What's up?"

Jordan didn't bother looking at the caller I.D. since it was the fifth-time Brianna had called her in the row.

"What are you doing best friend?" Jordan knew anytime Brianna referenced her as best friend that she wanted something.

"Chilling, watching T.V., why what's up?"

Jordan was dry with her greetings because she didn't want Brianna to ask her the very thing, she fixed her mouth to ask.

"Do you want to go out with me tonight? It's on me." Jordan rolled her eyes like a pissed teen then replied.

"Not really, I really just want to chill like I'm doing. I'm tired, I been doing a lot of running around for Jasmine." Jordan's lie came effortless.

"Friend, I really need you tonight. I got so much going with me. I swear I'm not going to make it without you."

Jordan pulled the phone away from her mouth then sucked her teeth like a spoiled brat. "Damn, I don't feel like this shit," she murmured before placing the phone back to her face, "Where are you trying to go, Brianna? I don't feel like being bothered with a big crowd."

"We don't have to go to no club or nothing, I just want to hit up a bar scene, or let's go to the Daiquiri Factory," she suggested in her kiddy voice.

"Oh alright, I'll hang for a minute but I'm not staying long." Jordan hated having a big heart. Sometimes she wished she just didn't care as much as she did.

"Okay, we don't have to stay long." Brianna knew once she got Jordan out of the house, she was good. Jordan always recited the same lines whenever Brianna needed her to go out but always did the complete opposite.

Jordan was a protector by nature, and she always felt obligated to look after Brianna, and Brianna knew how to play on her weakness to get what she wanted.

"I'll meet you there in like twenty minutes, and don't have me waiting! I will leave your ass." Jordan hung her cell up before Brianna could respond and fetched something to wear.

After thirty minutes of preparation, Jordan finally left the house. She didn't bother leaving on time because she knew how Brianna rolled, and she rolled in late. The Atlanta nights were cool, and the streets were clear, so it took Jordan no time to get to midtown from the old Grady Homes apartments. She walked in like a saint who was out of place.

She gripped onto her Juicy couture bag as she walked through the tight crowds of gays who were bustling in conversations over slushy

daiquiris. Jordan gawked at the room for a table that she and Brianna could sit at. She circled the room with her eyes, but the place was packed.

"Jordan?" Brianna called out from the balcony. "I'm over here." Jordan lowered her eyes to get a better vision of Brianna.

"Oh, I didn't know you were here already. I knew for sure you would be late."

"No, I told you I wouldn't be." Jordan could see that Brianna had started the party without her. Her eyes were fiery red and she already had one empty cup on the table and another half full in her hand. "You are looking refreshed, best friend." Brianna's words slurred. Jordan pulled out her chair and rested her bag in her lap.

"You started without me, I, see?" Jordan said.

"Yeah, had to. You were taking too long." Brianna sipped more of the green-yellow mixed daiquiri. "Did I interrupt your late-night booty call?"

Jordan didn't know how to answer Brianna. She wasn't sure if she had heard something or was just drunk. "What booty call, what are you talking about?"

Brianna burst into laughter and after three seconds Jordan joined; it was safe to say that Brianna was just drunk.

"Girl, your ass better get you some dick!" Brianna's voice sounded over Rihanna's Pour It Up.

"Lower your voice," Jordan demanded.

"Girl, we're in a damn bar. Who whispers in a bar, Jordan?" Brianna's behavior made it clear to Jordan that she was past drunk. "What are you drinking today?" Brianna cracked a crooked smile.

"Shit, everything," she answered before sipping the last of her drink. "Where the hell is that damn waitress? I need me another drink."

Brianna's neck had a permanent swivel in it. She looked around the bar for a waitress. "You don't need any more drinks, honey."

"Jordan, I do, friend. I'm telling you; I'm going to break into pieces if I don't take my mind off all this shit that's brewing." As Jordan called for the waitress, Brianna buried her head on the table, trying to conceal her tears.

"Brianna, maybe you don't need to take your mind off your problems but find a solution to them."

Brianna sat up and whipped her tears, staring in the opposite direction of Jordan. "You right, I do need to find me a solution, but I just don't know where to start." Brianna tried to catch her tears, but she failed; her tears showered down her cheeks uncontrollably.

"I'm so broken right now, Jordan. I don't know what to do. I feel like I'm dealing with too much at once."

Jordan's heart wanted to surrender but she was too far in now. She knew if she told Brianna the truth it would only destroy her, plus it would be the end of a ten-year friendship. There was no way Brianna could forgive Jordan. She was always about that fighting-life when it came to her men.

"What's bothering you? Is it Skylar?" Jordan played the clueless role well.

After a silent five minutes, Brianna responded.

"He left me, Jordan. The mother fucker left me when I needed him most." Jordan shook her head no in shame.

"I don't know what to say to that, Brianna. I know there's nothing I can say that will make you feel better." The pretty bi-racial waitress walked over to the table.

"Is everything okay over here? Do you girls need anything else?"

"As a matter of fact, we do, can you bring us two of whatever she had?" Jordan pointed at Brianna's empty cup.

"Sure, will that be all?"

"Yes, that will be all for now." Jordan rubbed Brianna on the arm. "Is there anything I can do?" she asked.

"Yeah, tell me you told me so. At least I'll know it wasn't me but that bastard who ruined a good thing." Jordan cracked a smile to lighten the mood.

"Now you know it was that bastard who ruined yawl. What did he say was the reason for him leaving?" Brianna grabbed the drinks out of the waitress hands before she could even seat them down.

"Y'all let me know if you need anything else," the waitress said before she walked off.

"It doesn't even matter why he left." Brianna resumed the conversation after she had a sip of her drink. "I can tell you this, that mother fucker gon' regret it."

Brianna was too embarrassed to tell Jordan that Emerson had no good reason for leaving, so she skipped around that fact.

"Hell, yeah he gon' regret it, you're good to him." Jordan's words tasted like shit. She hated the person she was betraying, but she had no other option.

"I'm talking about that nigga gone feel it. I sold all his shit: clothes, shoes, and jewelry. Oh, yeah and his car's gone, some niggas in the hood stole it."

The warm smile on Brianna face was evidence that she wasn't joking around. Jordan's heart dropped to her stomach. She knew Emerson was going to be pissed once he heard the news.

"Girl, you better hope that damn man doesn't press charges." Brianna burst into laughter again.

"I'm not worried about that nigga! I'm gonna go up to his job tomorrow and stir some shit up." Jordan shook her head no.

"Don't do that, Brianna."

"What the hell you mean, don't do that? That nigga hurt me to my core. I mean, I know that's not how you roll, Jordan, but I can't take the high road like you; I want that nigga to feel what I feel inside."

"Where he works anyway?" Jordan was always curious where Emerson got his money from. She assumed he was a drug dealer of some sort since he kept large amounts of cash on him.

"He works for his daddy's jewelry company. He's an heiress kid so he's not going to get fired. I just want to piss his parents off since they never liked me anyway." Jordan burst into laughter.

"Well, if it makes you feel better, then do your thang." The girls laughed some more.

"Well, you know I got to go, it's getting late and I'm tired." Jordan swallowed the last of her drink.

"Is Jasmine all right? She hasn't got back sick or nothing, has she?"

"Oh no, she's fine. Her numbers are high. I just had to take her to get some things for the cheerleader competition." Jordan forgot all about the lie she told earlier but she covered up good. "Are you going to be able to make it home?" Brianna stood up like a professional drinker.

"Yeah, girl, I'm good. It's gonna take more than some damn daiquiris to get me wasted." The girls gave each other warm, tight hugs before parting ways.

"Text me when you make it home," Jordan screamed out.

"I will, drive safe." Brianna responded before jumping in her jeep.

# 13

---

Cigars and cigarettes perfumed the pool hall. Jordan stood still in the middle of the floor gawking the room out for Emerson.

"Hey there, sweet thing. Who're you looking for?" The white man with the rusty smile spoke loudly over Katy Perry's Black Horse.

"Oh, I'm looking for Emerson," Jordan responded.

"Who honey? You going to have to speak up!" he asked.

"I said, I'm looking for Emerson."

"Oh, you looking for Emerson; well, why didn't you say so? He's right over there by the tables, taking them young men's money." he joked.

Jordan tried to wash away her cheesy smile before reaching Emerson, but she couldn't. Seeing him play pool with his tight ass tooted in the air made her blush.

"For a minute there I almost believed you knew what you were doing," Jordan whispered in Emerson's ear from behind.

"Girl, don't be rolling up on me like that, you could get yourself hurt." Emerson was only teasing Jordan. He had smelled her scent before

she even whispered one word in his ear. "Yo, Rodger!" Emerson waved at the young hillbilly with his pool stick. "You can finish this game on

me; I'm going to go have me a drink." Emerson led Jordan to the dinette booth.

"You hungry?" he asked.

"Yeah, a little, I really didn't get to eat much with Brianna."

Emerson opened the food menu with a frown pasted on his face, "Oh, so that's why you couldn't answer my call. I must have called you about a million times."

Jordan knew the attitude was coming sooner or later, since she ignored three of his calls while out with Brianna.

"I was with her, what you want me to do?"

The hard, hot air releasing from Emerson's mouth was clear evidence that he was beyond frustrated.

"I don't know what you're supposed to do. That's something you need to figure out and quick! I'm doing my part and I did it without asking for one instruction from you." Jordan set up tall and cleared her voice.

"First off, I'm gon' need for you to watch your voice. I have one father not many, and I don't take orders from him. You know the situation we're in is sticky. Do you or do you not?"

Jordan's eyes stalked Emerson's but he still ignored her question. "Well sit there like a damn dummy then, but don't talk that shit to me. I'm not Brianna and I'm not your daughter. I just can't be cold-hearted to the girl like you would like me to. She's been my friend for ten years. You've been my friend for only a couple of weeks."

"Can you bring the wings-and-thing platter and a corona please?" Emerson asked the thin Caucasian lady.

"Sure, will that be all for you?"

"Yeah, and whatever she's having," he added with a nasty wave towards Jordan.

"I'll have the wings and shrimp salad and make that a coke on ice; thank you." Jordan and Emerson's eyes met and the two both cracked a smile shaking their heads no.

"What am I going to do with you?" He asked.

"I don't know; I'm the one who should be asking that question." The two bursts into laughter for five short seconds before Emerson changed the tone.

"But for real Jordan, you got to let her go or let her know or both if we are going to work out baby girl. You cannot have your cake and eat it too." Jordan stared off into space. She knew what Emerson was saying had truth to it, but she just wasn't ready to face the truth so early on.

"I haven't even been around her that much, but she called me crying, talking about she needed to talk, so I went." Emerson shook his head once more. "Why are you shaking your head, looking at me like that?" she asked. "Because you just don't get it. You don't get what I'm telling you." Emerson took his beer out of the waitress's hands before she could place it on the table. "Thank you, sweetheart."

"Oh, you're welcome and your food is on its way." "Cool," he said.

"Let me taste some of your beer," Jordan joked, attempting to change the tone of their night.

"Go head on, you don't even damn drink. You're not about to waste my beer."

And just like a toddler with lips poked out, Emerson fell weak to Jordan's charm.

"I'm not going to play over it, I just want to taste it. I need to see what the hype's about." Jordan flashed her beautiful warm smile and Emerson was hypnotized.

"Here, silly, take a sip and don't backwash in my shit either." They laughed, then Jordan swallowed a mouthful of Corona. "How does it taste?" he asked.

"It's not bad, not my preference but it's not bad."

"How do you even know what's your preference if you don't even drink?" Emerson swallowed down half of the beer in a gulp.

"I like sweet-tasting alcohol; you know like wine or wine coolers, or daiquiris, drinks like that."

"Yeah, you look like a wine drinker. I'm going have to take you to a wine vineyard one day."

"Yeah, that would be nice," she responded before sipping on her coke. "So, do you want to know what I found out today about your ex?" Jordan's question broke the ten-second silence.

"Not really but what?" Jordan cracked a smile, flashing her deep left dimple.

"What, why are you laughing?" He asked.

"Emerson, promise not to be pissed when I tell you."

"I can't promise you that, now tell me what you found out. All this suspense shit is what's pissing me off."

After sixty long seconds, Jordan finally broke her silence. "Brianna sold all of your jewelry and clothes."

"What!" he snapped. "You better be playing with me, Jordan, for that bitch's sake. My fucking jewelry cost more than her life." Jordan's heart dropped to her stomach and at that moment she regretted saying anything to Emerson about her and Brianna's conversation.

"Are you playing with me right now, Jordan, like for real are you fucking with me right now?"

"You promised you wouldn't get mad." Emerson swallowed the last corner of his beer.

"I didn't promise your ass anything and sitting right here laughing at this shit like it's funny to you, Jordan." He jumped up from the booth and dropped forty dollars on the table.

"Where are you going, Emerson? Come back now, for real." Jordan tried pulling Emerson back by his Ralph Lauren shirt, but he tugged away.

"Emerson, don't you go do nothing stupid boy! She's not even at home anyway!" she screamed out to get his attention.

"Where the hell she is then?" Emerson doubled back and Jordan flinched.

"She is staying at some hotel."

"Don't worry I know exactly where she's at," he mumbled on his way out the door.

Jordan's palms began to sweat. She instantly became a nervous wreck. She sat in the booth biting down on her fingernails, watching as Emerson exited the pool hall. She didn't know what to expect. Emerson's actions could easily expose her betrayal if he weren't careful about the words he chose, and judging from his attitude, he had no control over his temper.

Any, if not everything about his and Jordan's involvement could easily slip out.

# 14

---

Mary J. Blige's I'm going down softly played on Brianna's Samsung Galaxy while tropical rain forest Bath and Body Work candles fragranced the hotel room. She had cried all she could cry, and she finally just wanted a moment of peace. She slid the sweet-scented lotion up and down her legs slowly, hoping the massage would release her stress. Boom, Boom, Boom! The knocks on the door startled Brianna. She rubbed the rest of the lotion in and wrapped the robe around her tight.

"Who is it?" she asked, standing at the room door.

"Room services."

Brianna could hear the crack in Emerson's voice. She cracked a smile and replied, "I didn't order room service," Brianna blushed. I knew his ass would come back, she thought before opening the door.

"What you want fool---?" Plaw! Emerson greeted Brianna with his fist as soon as she opened the door.

"You stupid bitch!" Brianna covered her face with her forearm. "Where the fuck is my shit?" Emerson's size eleven *Nike* slammed into Brianna's rib cage. "Bitch I will kill you in this motherfucker if you don't get to talking!" Brianna attempted to pull her hair out of Emerson's hands with one hand and she continued to cover her face with the other.

"Let go of my hair Emerson!" she cried out.

"I'm going to ask you one more time bitch: where is my shit at?" One of Emerson's fists pounded into Brianna's face and the other one yanked on her beautiful sew-in. "You stupid bitch, I hope you use that money for protection, bitch, because you just wrote your obituary with that stupid move."

Brianna ducked and jumped every time Emerson spoke. After ten minutes of brutally beating her, he stood over her like a beast at war.

"You're going to jail, you bastard! I swear you are," Brianna sobbed out as Emerson walked toward the door. "you say what? You say something to me bitch? Speak up!" Emerson doubled back and Brianna's heart dropped to her stomach.

"Say it again bitch, let me hear you?" Emerson's voice carried. Brianna kept her head bowed, tucked away between her knees, as she felt Emerson looing over her,"

"That's what I thought bitch," Paw! Agunk of Emerson's saliva rested in Brianna's hair, and some sprinkled all over her forearm. Brianna's sobbing increased as soon as she heard the door close. She picked her phone and dialed nine-one-one.

"9-1-1 emergency, what's your emergency?"

Brianna rocked back and forth sobbing loud into the phone, trying to control her crying with snot running down her nose.

"I was sobbing, just---jumped--on sniffing, by my boyfriend!" Brianna cried out.

"Is he still there?"

"No, he's gone."

"We're sending help out to you now. Are you at the Marriot hotel?" Brianna sniffed for a long ten seconds before she answered.

"Yes, room 203."

"Okay stay put, and help will be on the way."

"APD, is everybody okay?" The Atlanta police yelled into the room. The door was cracked open. Emerson had never shut it behind him, and Brianna had never left her spot.

"Ma'am, is he still here?" Brianna shook her head no, sniffing uncontrollably.

"Ma'am, can you tell me what happened?" Slowly, Brianna held her head up to eye the police and there was no explaining needed. The evidence was written on her face.

"Ma'am, who did this to you?" Brianna rubbed her hands through her hair, trying to control her sobbing so she could answer the officer.

"It was my boyfriend. He found where I was hiding and came to jump on me. He doesn't want me to leave him, and he jumped on me when he found me." Her lies came effortlessly.

"What is his name, ma'am, so we can put a warrant out on him?" Brianna hesitated and the police shook his head.

"Do you want to press charges or not?" Brianna knew her hesitation made the cop want Emerson's name more.

"His name Emerson Waters but I don't know where he went because he's not staying at our condo anymore," she answered, wiping the snot from her nose.

"Don't worry about that, we will find him. I want you to go down to the station in the morning and press charges.

"What's your name?" he asked, writing down Emerson's name on his notebook.

"I'm Brianna Braxton," she responded, scooting up off the floor onto the bed.

"Brianna, once you go down to the station and press charges, we will send a detective out to you. In the meantime, I'll look and see if I can pick him up off the streets. What kind of car does he drive?"

"Well, he has several but one of them is black seven forty-five and he has a burgundy Porsche truck as well. I'm not sure which one he was driving though."

The handsome cop, whose badge read Mr. Bailsmen, continued to write down the information given.

"Do you know the tag number to any of these cars?"

Brianna's eyes fixated on the ceiling as she tried to think of one of the tag numbers, but she couldn't.

"I'm sorry, I can't think of one," she sobbed.

"Don't worry about it, I'll use what I have here. Don't you cry, we'll get to the bottom of this." Officer Bailsman rubbed Brianna on the shoulders. "It's going to be okay; you just stay as far away from him as possible and if he calls, try to record his conversation." Brianna slowly wiped her eyes and nose.

"Okay, I will." Her tone was sweet and innocent.

"Okay, that's all I need from you today. Remember to get down to the station in the morning." Brianna followed the officer to the door.

"Thanks for your help," she said to him before closing the door. Brianna slid her back down the door the wall until her bottom was on the floor.

She began to think about her carelessness. How could she forget quickly about the damage she's done to his things? "Damn! He must've been out to the condo to get his things." She laughed, rubbing the blood off her bottom lip.

"That's okay. I'll get the last laugh," she mumbled before diving into the queen bed with high hopes of sleeping all of her problems and stress away.

# 15

The new smell of fresh, clean hardwood floors and new paint perfumed the house. The girls twirled in circles like they were shooting a movie.

"It's so big, Jordan!" Jasmine walked from room to room, touring the beautiful bungalow-styled home. "Your new boo must have that paper." Jordan's perfectly arched left eyebrow raised.

"Where you get that slang from, honey?" she asked Jasmine with a shocked expression pasted to her face.

"I mean; you know? He must be doing well for himself?" Jasmine quickly fixed her tone.

"Yeah, he does well. He's in the jewelry business with his father." Jordan stood center stage in the room that she had nominated for Jasmine's room. "So, do you like this one or the other one?" Jordan asked. "I love this one."

"I thought you would like this one better." Jordan walked into the beautiful closet. "This closet is almost as big as the master bedroom closet."

"I know, it's so beautiful. The entire house is just beautiful. Like I can't believe we're going to be living here." The smile glued to Jordan's

face was a proud one; she loved the fact that she could give Jasmine a better upbringing than she and her sister had had.

"Now this is the thing, Jasmine. I'm not letting go of our apartment. I'm going to keep it just in case we need it again. You know we can never be too sure."

Jasmine admired her aunt's strength. It was a talent her mother Rosa lacked. Jasmine would often joke with her aunt about taking all the strength from her mother, but Jordan assured her every time the joke came to the forefront that strength wasn't easy to come by.

"Okay, aunt, so do we tell him or nah?" Jasmine asked, posing with duck lips.

"Nah, this could be our little secret. We'll just let him think we got rid of the place, but you go there after school and that's where I'll pick you up from." Jasmine nodded yes in agreement.

"That's a bet," she responded.

"And where did you get so ghetto, honey?" Jasmine burst into laughter.

"I'm not ghetto, aunt. You're just boogie."

"Is that a fact?"

"That's a fact, but it's clear to me now, though." Jordan stepped out of the closet and shut the door. She had to give this conversation her undivided attention.

"What's clear to you now?" Jordan asked, fixating her eyes on Jasmine in hopes of reading her truth.

"It's clear to me why you weren't interested in Coach. At first, I just thought you were being a stuck-up snob." Giggles.

"Excuse me?" Jordan asked.

"I did, aunt, you know you can be really hard on men sometimes. "And that's what I thought you were doing but all along you had you a cookie baking in the oven." Jordan couldn't hold on to her serious face, she burst into laughter. Jasmine wasn't far from wrong, and Jordan knew it.

"Yes, I was talking to someone at the time when you and your aunt tried to play matchmaker." Jordan's Kool-Aid smile was evidence that she was basking in love.

"But it's complicated, so I don't want you telling nobody just yet. Not even your aunt Brianna, okay?" Jasmine picked up on the shift in Jordan's tone and instinctively responded without hesitation.

"Yes, I understand; it's between me and you." The air Jordan released un-tensed her body.

"Good. So, what do you want to do first, unpack then eat or eat then unpack?" Jasmine stared off into space with a smirk on her face.

"I think it would be smart if we to unpack first because if I eat, I might get the black folk disease." Sniggers. "Sounds like a plan," Jordan said.

"So where is this mystery man? Is he coming to help us unpack or nah?"

"Well, he had to get some things straightened with his last place, so he only had time to bring me the keys, but he'll help out later, you'll meet him."

Jasmine followed Jordan out of the room and into the seating area where the boxes rested.

"Is he okay with me moving in with you guys?"

"Yeah, baby, he knows you are my first love and that he can only be second runner-up." Jordan spoke as if she was a thirty-something-year-old woman.

"Okay, I just didn't want to be in the way of your happiness." Jasmine's soft tone weakened Jordan's heart.

"Girl don't be silly. You know family is always first." Jordan reached into her clutch to answer her vibrating cell. "What's up chic?"

"This nigga went bizarre on me last night, girl!" Jordan wasn't prepared for Brianna's dramatic response. Her eyes widened and her heart sank to her stomach.

"What! What you mean he went bizarre?" Jordan's voice echoed throughout the empty house.

"Where are you?" Brianna asked after hearing the echo.

"I'm handling some things with Jasmine." Jasmine eyed Jordan with her duck lips poked out when she heard her aunt lie.

"Oh, but can you come hang out with me for a while? I really need a friend right now." Jasmine was all ears to the conversation once she noticed her aunt's frustration.

"I can't just drop what I'm doing and come to your rescue Brianna. What the hell happened?"

"He fucking beat me, Jordan! The mother fucker beat the shit out of me." Brianna broke into intense sobbing.

"He beat you up?"

"Yes, he went fucking crazy girl!"

"See, I told you that wasn't a good fucking ideal man. How he found out?" Jordan asked, curious to see if she was exposed or clear.

"I think he must have gone to the condo and seen his things gone or something?" Jordan released hot, hard air once again.

"Shit, Brianna! You got to come on man and get your shit together. I got enough shit on my plate." Brianna began to sob louder.

"I'm sorry if my life's too fucked up for you to give a shit in your busy perfect life!" She sniffed.

"nobody said that, Brianna. I'm just tired and I got a plateful already. Jasmine and I will meet you at Hooters in like an hour."

"Okay," sniveling. "Call me when you leave." Brianna knew there was no way Jordan could say no to her crying.

"Yeah, I'll call you when we're on the way."

"Okay, yawl leaving now?" Jordan's eyes rolled like a teen being sent to the principal's office in high school.

"No, I'll call you when we leave. Let us finish up what we're doing here." Jordan's attitude was loud, and Brianna didn't want to upset her, so she agreed with Jordan's plan, instead of pushing for Jordan to leave immediately like she had originally planned.

"Okay, call me when you leave," she repeated.

"Okay." Jordan slid her phone back into her clutch.

"What's going on, aunt? Is Aunt Brianna, okay?"

"Yeah, she good; do you want some Hooters for dinner?"

"Yeah, that sounds good to me."

"Okay, well let's go grab something to eat. Your aunt is going through a crisis." Jasmine followed Jordan out the door.

# 16

The Cîroc and pineapple mixture twirled around the ice cubes as Brianna's shaky hands rattled the glass. She sat silently, staring in the blank air, patiently waiting for Jasmine and Jordan to arrive. She could hardly wait to tell Jordan how right she was about the man she despised: Emerson Waters.

After twenty minutes, the girls finally arrived.

"Sorry we're late. There's so much traffic down here and then on top of that, it's almost impossible to find a parking spot." Jordan hugged Brianna tightly from her stool since she didn't bother standing.

"Hey, Aunt Brianna."

Brianna continued to stare blankly into space as if neither Jordan nor Jasmine was speaking to her. Trying to grasp on to her patience, Jordan attempted to ignore Brianna's diva attitude and continued with a healthy tone. "Have you ordered anything, sister?"

Brianna's quaking legs rattled the table. She tapped on the glass with her fake nails, looking into space as if no one was talking to her.

"Look, I don't have time for this shit!" Jordan said before snatching up her purse and lifting it from the table. "You are sitting here like you

don't hear anybody talking to you. I got enough shit on my plate! I can't babysit a grown-ass woman."

Brianna snatched her black knock-off Sentra's away from her face. "Look at my face!" Brianna snapped with tears dripping from her purple eyes and down her swollen cheeks. "I mean, damn, Jordan, what's up!" Jordan just stared at Brianna's face, speechless. She couldn't figure out if Brianna was just being dramatic Brianna or if Emerson had blown her cover.

"What the hell are you talking about, and what the hell happened to your face?" Jordan asked, sitting back in her seat next to Jasmine.

"That's what I'm trying to figure out: what the hell happened?"

If Jordan's blouse wasn't buttoned up pass her chest, Brianna would see how hard Jordan's heart was beating. Jordan knew that Brianna knew, she was the only person she told about destroying Emerson's things. Jordan sat quietly, shaking her head no in disappointment, trying not to assume that Brianna had pieced the puzzle together. She knew better than to tell on herself, so she pretended to be quiet, waiting on Brianna to go on about what she knew or speculated.

"I don't know who this nigga is no more. I can't figure out for the life of me what the hell happened between us." Silently Jordan exhaled. She was now clear for take-off.

"Now you know damn well that relationship has been on ice for quite some time now, Brianna. Honestly, I think you were just hanging on to what you thought y'all could be together and ignoring what the two of you really were."

Brianna nodded her head, then her tears began to pour from her swollen eyes like water poured from a faucet.

"I needed to hear you say it because that is the only thing that makes sense to me."

Jasmine didn't know Brianna's entire story but considering her eyes, she could only imagine what she must have felt like. Brianna caught Jasmine staring at her then said, "Don't give no nigga your heart, you hear me? No nigga is worthy. They all lie, cheat, and most of fucking all, use your heart as a doormat."

Jordan so badly wanted to interrupt Brianna's chant to Jasmine, as she felt she shouldn't be scared so early about something that can be so beautiful, but she just kept quiet and allowed Brianna to have her moment. She felt it was the least she could do since she had opened her mouth and blasted Brianna's secret to Emerson.

"So why did he hit you this time, Brianna?" Jordan asked after sipping some of Brianna's drink.

"This time was completely different from the others, Jordan."

Brianna knew from Jordan's left eyebrow rising that she had no sympathy for her situation. "I know what you are thinking Jordan," Brianna interrupted her explanation to say.

"I mean I'm not judging you, but I just don't understand why you're so surprised he hit you; it's not like it's the first-time Brianna. You have been allowing him to do this for quite some time now." Brianna's tears increased.

"I don't care if you want to say I told you so, in fact go ahead if it makes you feel better because I agree with you," Brianna added.

"I'm not trying."

The thin Hooter's waitress came with menus and Jordan paused her response.

"Here are your menus, ladies, can I get you girls something to drink?" the waitress, Sarah, asked.

"Yes, as a matter of fact you can get us all the strongest margaritas you have," Jasmine joked.

"I know that's right, niece," Brianna said.

"They're obviously delusional." Jordan spat.

Sarah couldn't make out if Jordan was playing or serious, so she pasted a fake smile on her face and asked Jordan once more.

"So, what would you like to drink, ma'am?"

"You can bring me a margarita, but you can bring her,"

Jordan pointed at Jasmine, rolling her eyes with her duck lips poked out, "a Sierra Mist."

"Okay, and do you know what you are having, or do you need time?" Sarah asked Jordan.

"Yeah, actually I already know. I'll have the crab leg bucket and twenty wings hot and naked. That will be for the both of us."

"Okay, I will get right back, and your food is on the way, ma'am."

Sarah turned to Brianna and said, "Would you like another drink?"

"Yeah, that will be great."

Jordan waited until Sarah was out of sight, then she resumed her response. "Like I was saying, Brianna, I'm not trying to garnish bragging

rights here; I just want you to be happy and I know if you keep lying to yourself, there is no way that's going to happen."

Brianna said nothing. She just listened like a patient at therapy.

"I know you think you love him but I'm more convinced that you are just in love with what you think you could have had with him." Brianna remained silent; she just nodded her head yes. "I hate to be the person who has to tell you these things, because it seems like I hate on you when really all I want is the best for you."

"I don't see it as hate, Jordan. I know you care for me like a sister; that's the only reason why I listen to you."

Since when do you listen to me Brianna, really?

Jordan thought, taking her drink from Sarah's hand before she could even sit it down.

"Just let the girl who can deal with Emerson's ass deal with Emerson's ass." Jasmine's eyes widened but neither of the girls noticed.

Isn't Emerson her aunt's new boo? Ooh hell, she thought.

"Girl, trust me, I'm done with that mother fucker. You don't have to tell me anymore. I'm not taking Emerson's ass back after this shit."

Jordan side-eyed Brianna. She spoke like she was the one leaving Emerson, but Jordan knew better. Emerson had let Jordan listen to the voicemails Brianna left begging Emerson to take her back. Jordan knew if Emerson was still in her life, she wouldn't even be bothered with her.

Everything she and Brianna did together revolved around Emerson and her schedule. Thinking about how selfish Brianna was with their friendship when she was involved with Emerson made Jordan feel no remorse for her recent decisions.

After an hour of talking about old times and future goals, the girls finally decided to call it a night.

Jasmine turned down K Michelle's Can't Raise a Man, and finally grew the balls to ask her aunt what she had been curious about all night. "Aunt, if I ask you something, you promise you won't get mad?" Jasmine knew that putting her baby-soft tone on would smooth her aunt over.

"Yeah, what is it?" Jordan answered.

"You got to promise you won't get mad first."

"Jasmine, I don't have time to play games with you; ask me or don't ask me," Jordan snapped.

"Okay, here it is. Is your new boo Aunt Brianna's old boo?"

Jordan's eyes widened. She felt like she had just got caught having sex in front of her child. "If I give this answer, you must take it to your grave, deal?" Jordan replied.

"Deal," Jasmine answered.

"Yes." Jasmine inhaled air like she was an asthma patient.

"But you cannot tell anyone." Jasmine nodded her head yes with her eyes wide. "I know what it may look like to you, but it's not like that," Jordan explained. "You don't have to explain to me. You're my aunt. I'm with you no matter what. Family is always first. I'm just glad you found somebody." Jordan and Jasmine both burst into laughter.

"What'd you say?" Jordan asked.

"I'm serious, aunt, you haven't had a man in a long time. It's about time you got you one. You know... a shot at happiness." Speechless, Jordan couldn't say anything. Jasmine was growing into a fine girl, and she had no complaints. The way she carried herself spoke numbers about the lady she was growing into. "Well, I'm glad to have you by my side, little girl."

Jasmine burst into laughter once again. "I swear I forget you're like twenty-something. You act so much older," Jasmine said before turning the music back up.

# 17

The pleasing smell of Gain soap powder perfumed the house. Jordan pranced around in her lace boy shorts, singing aloud to Christina Aguilera, making sure all her chores were done before she left for the weekend.

"You're such a white girl. What the hell are you listening to?" Emerson asked, pressing himself against Jordan's soft ass.

"I am not a white girl, but this white girl can sing her ass off; hell, she sings like a black girl with soul." Jordan continued to fold the white clothes she had just taken from the dryer.

"Yeah, yeah, she still white," Emerson teased. "Why are you going to Miami again?" Emerson asked with his hands resting on his cut waist.

"I have told you this a million times." "So, tell me a million and one," he replied.

"It's something we do together as sisters every three months, we take trips.

That's why it's a sister support sister group." Emerson inhaled the Gain aroma from the white t-shirt when Jordan threw her hands up in the air.

"Only stuck-up bougie girls are a part of these types of groups," Emerson joked.

"I beg your pardon?" Jordan responded.

"It is okay, baby, I love you just the way you are." Both Jordan and Emerson burst into laughter at Emerson's comment. "No, for real, for real, I need a woman like you." Emerson's tone went from playful to serious in a heartbeat.

"Well,, you got me, so you better do the right thing." Jordan turned to face Emerson. He watched the light glisten off her brown eyes, then he slowly went in for a kiss, thrusting his tongue down her throat. "Emerson, I got something I want to tell you," Jordan pulled away from Emerson and said.

"Oh, Lord, this doesn't sound good. What is it?" he asked, stepping back so he could look her in her eyes.

"Well, I kind of made the decision a while ago that I was going celibate, and then I got with you and everything I stood for or had going on for myself kind of went out the window." Emerson shook his head no with his beautiful smile on display.

"Are you trying to tell me what I think you're trying to tell me?" Jordan blushed then responded with her fingers twirled up in front of her like a baby.

"Yes, I'm not having sex with you no more. I mean, at least until we are a union. That's what this trip is about." Emerson continued to shake his head in disbelief.

"Well that only means one thing," he responded.

"What?" she asked.

"I got to get what I can before you go to Miami." Emerson aggressively lifted Jordan onto the washer. Jordan could feel the head of his dick rubbing up against her impatient pussy. His body felt so good to her, she scooted to the end of the washer and pulled him in closer.

"You better make it count," she whispered into his ears before molesting his mouth with her wet kisses.

Emerson shoved his dick inside of Jordan, showing no mercy, "Aww!" she moaned. He heaved his dick deeper into her pussy then picked her up, carrying her to the folding bench while keeping his rhythm, bouncing her up and down on his steel on the way over.

"You sure you're not going to want no more of this?" he asked, laying Jordan on her back with her legs resting over his shoulders.

"I'm sure," she wailed.

"Wrong answer," he replied before digging a grave into her pussy with his large chocolate penis. "Who this pussy belongs to?" Emerson asked, pushing deeper into her walls.

"It belongs to you, Daddy." Jordan whined. After five long minutes of punishing Jordan, Emerson wanted to treat her,

"Turn over!" he demanded. She turned on her knees doggy style with her ass arched in the free air. He arched her back a little more then brought his mouth to meet her elevated pussy. He began a tongue expedition. His blazer tongue was a Taser gun. He had Jordan shaking for days. He electrocuted her pussy, and she came repeatedly. The two were so wrapped up in their love affair, they didn't notice Jasmine standing in the door with her cloth basket. She brought her clothes down for Jordan to wash like she'd asked, but she couldn't seem to walk away.

The way Emerson pleased Jordan was too stimulating. Watching them was better than any flick she and her friends had watched at slumber parties. Her little fourteen-year-old pussy began to tingle when Emerson began to suck the juices out of Jordan's ass. She was aware of oral on the pussy, but the ass was new to her. She softly set the basket down on the floor then shoved her two fingers deep into her leaking vagina.

The louder Jordan moaned the deeper Jasmine shoved her hands into her pussy. She wanted to feel what she was feeling so she pushed her fingers in harder and faster. No matter what she did she couldn't seem to make it happen the way Emerson did for Jordan. Frustrated, she left the basket by the door and went back to her room.

After Emerson finished sucking the juices out of Jordan, the two of them got into the sixty-nine position and devoured each other and after ten minutes of torture, Emerson couldn't take it anymore. He set Jordan on her knees and squirted his warm babies into Jordan throat.

"Aww, I see why your name is Jordan, girl, you got the gems," Emerson groaned, ejaculating all his seeds into Jordan's mouth.

Jordan opened her mouth wide so Emerson could see all his semen spread on her tongue then she swallowed it with much pleasure. Jordan slid back on her lace boy shorts and peeked out the door like a kid sneaking out the house. There was no Jasmine, but her clothes basket satin front of the laundry room door.

"Damn, do you think she heard us?" Jordan asked Emerson with her eyes bulk.

"Nah, that basket was there before we came in," Emerson answered.

"Oh, okay. Damn, I was about to say...." Jordan never said what she was about to say, she just smoothly walked out of the laundry room to get a shower, and Emerson followed behind.

# 18

The auditorium was packed with teens. Emerson shuffled his way through the crowd and to the bleachers with his popcorn and Sprite in tow. It had been ages since he attended a high school basketball game. He sat on the bleachers in front of the mean girls' clique and boy did he get an earful. They bickered about almost every girl that walked past, and nothing they had to say was pleasant.

"Who is the hunk on the first row?" The ringleader Ashley asked her friend, referring to Emerson.

"I don't know, but what I do know is he is fine as hell." Ashley turned her head so that Tara could read her face expression. "He's taken, thank you," Ashley replied with much attitude. Emerson snickered at the teens, shaking his head in disbelief. "Yes, they are way more mature than we were at that age."

The school nurse overheard the girls and noticed that Emerson did as well. "Yeah, they are way more mature than the girls I went to school with."

The beautiful nurse extended her hand out to Emerson for a proper greeting.

"I'm the school nurse, Ms. Walters," she said, shaking Emerson's hand.

"I'm Emerson, Emerson Waters," he replied.

"Oh okay, do you have a son here at Jackson High?"

"No, my niece is a cheerleader. I brought her here to cheer and I just decided to stay and watch the game."

Ms. Walters healthy jet-black bob bounced loosely as she slightly nodded her head up and down. "So, who is your niece?"

"Jasmine Brown," he answered.

"Oh, Jasmine is your niece, okay. I know her. I have to give her medicine sometimes."

Emerson caught Ms. Walter's eyes fixating on his broad chest and strong arms. She jumped quickly and turned away when his eyes meet her staring eyes.

"So, are you married?" She finally grew the balls to ask.

"Um, no, wow!" A crowd of teens ran out of the gymnasium and the distraction interrupted Emerson's answer.

He quickly jumped up and ran out of the gym behind the kids, along with other parents and teachers.

"You nasty ass bitch, I could beat the shit out of you, hoe, and not give a fuck in the world about the consequences!"

Emerson followed the loud bickering, pushing through the kids who were standing around for the show.

"I don't know what you are talking about; it wasn't me. You better go check your fucking black book bum ass, nigga!" Jasmine snapped back.

"Aye, aye, what the hell's going on?" Emerson interrupted.

"I'm about to beat this bitch, that's what's going on." Travis pulled on his crotch that was suffocating in the skinny jeans.

"Nah, you not going to do that. She's a girl, man. Calm down and have some respect," Emerson said, tapping Travis on the shoulders lightly.

"Man, she's no girl; she's a hoe!" "Oooh!" the crowd shouted.

"Look, I'm not going to keep allowing you to disrespect her. Now I'm trying to be nice." Emerson's patience began to thin out when he noticed the hurt in Jasmine's eyes.

"Travis Porter, you're working on a suspension if you keep it up." The girls' basketball coach yelled out as she broke up the crowd. "Everybody back into the gym or go home, your choice!" The male teachers and police enforcement assisted the coach with breaking up the crowd.

"I swear, bitch, this shit is not over. I'll see you around bitch, this shit not over!" Travis bumped Emerson then eyed him up and down like he was his equal.

"Trying to act like you don't know what's going on, nigga you know what's going on. She's your motherfucking niece. I'm going to have yawl mother fuckers locked up. Watch me if you think I'm bullshitting!" Emerson snickered than inhaled and exhaled, popping his knuckles. "Come on, Uncle Emerson, just let that fool talk. I'm not listening to anything he is saying. He's just mad because I broke up with him. He always tries to put on a show when there is a crowd around." Jasmine grabbed Emerson by his arm and led him out of the auditorium.

The ride over to the Ruth Chris was awkward and silent. Emerson didn't know what to say to Jasmine to smooth over what had happened at the game. He wasn't a father and his parenting skills, in his opinion, sucked. He treated Jasmine to her favorite restaurant, hoping it would make up for his lack of support. "Wow! These prices are crazy," Jasmine said staring at the menu.

"Oh, don't worry about that; just order what you want."

Emerson was in desperate need to make up for Jasmine. He felt responsible for her while Jordan was away and since he didn't knock the lights out of Travis for being so disrespectful towards her, he felt he had some major making up to do.

"Um, we're still deciding. Do you have any suggestions?" Emerson asked.

"Yeah, would y'all like to try our couple combos? It comes with steak, shrimp, lobster, and a bottle of our best wine."

The waitress spoke so fast it took a minute for Emerson to catch that she referred to them as a couple. "Wow! Did you just say a couple meal?" Jasmine burst into laughter at Emerson's reaction.

"I'm his niece, not his lady," Jasmine said.

"Oh, I'm so sorry, I didn't know," the waitress whose name tag read Carla responded.

"You alright, sweetheart, it's all good." Emerson closed his menu and said. "But I do like that meal choice."

"Yeah, me too, I mean except for the wine. You can bring me sweet tea instead." The waitress scooped up the menus.

"Okay, I'll be right back with y'all drinks."

"Oh boy, what a day," Emerson said, looking into his phone.

"Has my aunt called today?" Jasmine asked.

"Yeah, she called when you were cheering. I told her I would tell her to call you when we got home. Do you

want me to call her for you?"

"No that's okay," Jasmine snapped quickly.

"Oh, I see somebody don't want to get in trouble," Emerson teased.

"Yeah, she would just freak out and get all upset for nothing." Jasmine tapped her false nails on the table.

"So, what happened because I started to put the little nigga to sleep?"

Jasmine snickered then said, "I told you, I broke up with him because he always trying to show out on me. And when he saw, I wasn't trying to get back with him, he started making rumors up, talking about I gave him something."

Jasmine's beauty was undeniable, and Emerson knew the little boys had to be throwing themselves at her, so he told her what he would have told his daughter if he had one.

"Never allow a boy or a man to degrade or disrespect you. You're a beautiful girl and there's plenty of men who would die to have you as their girl."

Jasmine sat quietly listening to Emerson. She never had a father figure in her life, and it felt good to have a man's opinion on dating.

"You did the right thing by leaving his little ass alone and if he gives you any more trouble, it's going to take more than you pulling me out the gym to not get in his ass."

Jasmine snickered again. "I'm fine, my aunt raised a strong girl. She told me the day would come when boys would be angry at me for not doing what they want me to do, but that day will pass like every other bad day."

A proud smile was glued to Emerson's face. "Your aunt is raising you the right way. You so mature for your age and that's a good thing because we don't have to worry about you out here making stupid decisions."

Emerson and Jasmine enjoyed the night talking about everything under the sun. Jasmine expressed to Emerson how she is so happy that Jordan had him in her life and he expressed how he one day wanted to make her his wife.

# 19

The sound of the hard rain falling was music to Jasmine's ears. She could see the rain dwindling from the ceiling window in the shower. She cleaned her body like she hadn't showered in years. She was in heaven. Jordan had everything stocked in the walk-in shower: from shampoo to conditioner and the head on her shower had the hardest water pressure. Jasmine rubbed her fingers through her long silky and kinky textured hair once more, then finally, after twenty long minutes, got out of the shower.

She wrapped the white towel around her body tight, then tip-toed to her room across the hall. She didn't bother shutting her door since Emerson was relaxing in the living room watching ESPN. She turned her radio up so Beyoncé could sing over the sportscaster, which was echoing up the stairs.

Then she dropped her towel to the floor and stood naked in front of the fan, allowing the cool breeze to dry her body.

Jasmine rubbed her hands across her dripping wet body, singing aloud with Beyoncé's 1 plus 1.

"Make love to me," she said, massaging her clitoris, masturbating about Emerson. "Aww," she moaned when she pictured her fingers as his dick pushing into her.

"Um, make love to me, Emerson." She muttered, finger fucking her vagina like an experienced porn star. "Make love to me when my days look low, pull me in close and don't let me go," Jasmine sang so loud she didn't hear Emerson responding to her.

"What'd you say?" he said, screaming up the stairs, hoping he didn't have to get up. *Make love to me so when the world's at war, our love will heal us all,*" Jasmine continued to sing with one of her hands manipulating her kitty and the other falsifying her itty-bitty titties.

"What'd you say?"

Jasmine jumped at the sound of Emerson's voice, and he quickly shut the door. "I'm sorry, I thought I heard you calling me, I'm sorry, shit! I didn't see anything," he screamed, quickly running into his room and shutting the door behind him.

"Shit! Damn, what the hell is the girl in there doing?" Emerson murmured, pacing his room floor back and forth.

"It's okay." Jasmine walked into the master bedroom with the towel wrapped around her tight.

"I didn't see anything, I swear," Emerson responded.

"It's okay, I know you didn't." Jasmine stopped Emerson from pacing by gripping him by his muscular arms. "Calm down," she said softly, kissing him on his chest through his white beater.

Oh, shit, what's this girl doing? He thought as Jasmine seduced him. "Jasmine, what the hell are you doing?"

Jasmine ignored Emerson's aggression and continued to trail his body with her wet kisses. "Move girl; you done lost your damn mind." He pulled Jasmine away from him and headed for the door, but that didn't

stop her. She followed behind him. She quickly shut the door then dropped her towel.

"I won't tell, but I want you to take me and fuck me better than you have ever fucked anybody."

Emerson shook his head like Taz Mania, hoping to wake up from the nightmare. But when he re-opened his eyes, Jasmine's wet, naked body was still on display.

"Girl, you are fourteen years old. I would hurt you for one, and two I would go to jail, and three, your aunt will kill me. Now move!" Emerson tossed Jasmine's body to the side, and she quickly jumped back up in front of him.

"I told you, I won't tell," she repeated. "I'll protect you and I want you to hurt me if you can." Jasmine caressed Emerson's dick through his pants.

"Come on, what're you scared of?" she said, rubbing her nude body against his. "Take me, Emerson," she whispered in his ear with her hand massaging his growing dick.

"Uh, I feel him growing. Lay down, baby."

Emerson's mind might have been screaming no, but his dick had begun craving for her touch. She pushed him on the bed and rested back on his elbows as she unbuttoned his pants. Jasmine then began to run her fingers up and down the inside of his right thigh. Emerson looked at her, and she gave him the look he knew all too well. The look that tells him how much her body was yearning for his touch. After tussling with Emerson's belt buckle, Jasmine finally freed the Willy.

She blew cool air from her mouth onto the tip of his dick, teasing him. Her goal was to make him want it more than her, and it was working. The wait was killing Emerson; his pre-cum trickled down his dick.

"Um, somebody wants me, I see." Jasmine licked her lips slowly, staring Emerson directly in his eyes.

"If you don't suck this dick soon, I'm going to put you out." Jasmine didn't bother replying. She just slurped as much of Emerson's dick in one gulp as she could. She gagged a little, but it didn't stop her from trying to beat her aunt at the job. She deep throated his dick until she could feel his balls slamming up against her chin as she took it in and out of her warm mouth.

"Aww," Emerson shivered, his dick had never felt better. He leaned back with his hands covering his face, groaning as loudly as he could, enjoying his daytime dessert.

She pulled his pants down farther around his knees

and spread his legs, biting gently on his kneecaps as she worked her way up to his balls. She carefully took his ball sack into her mouth and then suckled on it, contracting her cheek muscles around it. She sucked long and hard. She had never sucked on a man's dick before, only boys and that mixed with the excitement that he was her aunt's man turned her on. Jasmine had never felt so grown-up in her life.

After shooting a mouthful of semen into Jasmine's mouth, Emerson was ready to bust her new pussy wide open. He got up and demanded, "Get on the bed." Jasmine obeyed, got up and laid flat on her back.

"No, on your knees," he said, turning her around doggy style. He slid his hands from her ass to her pussy, finger fucking them both, preparing them for what was about to come.

"Are you a virgin?" he asked.

"No, but my ass is," she responded with her ass arched in the air.

"Not anymore." Emerson shoved his dick into Jasmine's ass with no mercy. He wanted to give her what she begged for, and since she was giving him a free pussy, he was going to treat her like she treated herself: like trash. He fucked her ass until it burned.

"Aww, wait a minute, it hurts. Go slow," she cried out. Emerson ignored her request and fucked the bottom out her ass while finger fucking her pussy with four of his fingers.

"Tell me to go deeper," he demanded.

"No, go slower," she cried.

"Wrong response," Emerson replied before shoving as much of his large dick into her ass.

"Aww!"

Tears were running from Jasmine eyes. She couldn't bear the pain. She screamed but no one could hear her. They were home alone.

"Aww, you done started something now, girl," Emerson groaned. "You're going to get this dick every time it's hard."

Jasmine bawled but no one could hear her. After five minutes of punishing Jasmine's ass, Emerson took his dick out and dug a grave into her pussy, shoving his four fingers in her ass.

"Um, this little pussy belongs to me now. Shit, it's good too!" Emerson moaned. "Thank you, Jasmine."

Jasmine could taste the blood off her bottom lip she bit down on it so hard. "Who you belong to, Jasmine?" Emerson asked, aggressively pounding his dick into the back of her walls.

"If you don't answer me little bitch, I'll stick my dick and my balls in your ass." "I belong to you, Emerson. "I'll do whatever you want me to. Just don't fuck my ass no more," she bawled, but Emerson didn't listen. He took advantage of Jasmine's innocence and weakness and did just what he wanted to with her for the rest of the weekend. He fucked everything from her mouth to her ass whenever he wanted to.

Emerson didn't want to disrespect Jordan, so he slept in Jasmine's room for the remainder of the weekend. Anytime he thought his dick was hard, he would shove into one of Jasmine's holes without permission. The control he had over her felt good; he felt like the man. Jasmine would wake up in the middle of the night with his dick on her lips and not say a word. She knew what to do and without any fuss she did it. In just a day and half, Emerson had mind-fucked Jasmine so good, she was his little puppy. When he said jump, she asked how high.

# 20

The whizzing noise the doctor's bed made from Jasmine's shaking legs wrecked Jordan nerves. She snapped, "Stop shaking that damn bed, girl! Why are you all shaky and shit?" Before Jasmine Jones could give a response, the doctor re-entered the room.

"Well, your numbers look good. I guess somebody has been keeping up with their meds." Jasmine smiled like an angel.

"And what's the results on the other checkups?" Jordan impatiently asked.

"Well, I'll let Jasmine talk to you about that." If Jasmine's face expression could speak, it would say busted.

"Well, I know what that means. So, is she pregnant?" Jordan snapped.

"Um, that's something you have to talk to Jasmine about as well, but before you do, I need to speak to her alone if you don't mind."

Jordan jumped up from her seat and snatched her purse that rested on the arm of the chair.

"These laws and rules are the reason we have so many teens running around pregnant. I just don't get how I can't know what's going with the teen I'm raising," Jordan barked before slamming the door behind her.

Jasmine secretly thanked God for the confidential law between teens and their doctors. "Now that we are alone

Ms. River, is it anything you'd like to tell me or ask?"

"No, well yes. Am I pregnant?" Jasmine asked quickly.

"No, you can relax; you're not pregnant, Jasmine." Doctor Jones's words felt like a knife stabbing Jasmine in the heart. A part of her wanted to be pregnant; she yearned for the chance to love a baby better than her mother loved her.

"Were you expecting to be pregnant?" Doctor Jones asked.

"No, I just asked because you said you had something to talk to me about," Jasmine snapped.

"Well yes, I do, I have some questions I'll like to ask you. For starters, now that you are sexually active, are we using protection?"

Jasmine rolled her eyes looking away, up to the ceiling before answering, "Yes." "Okay, you don't have to be bothered by my questions; I'm only asking them for your sake, Jasmine, okay?" Jasmine didn't bother replying. She sat on the bed with her feet dangling.

"I guess my next question is would you like to get on some birth control?"

"No, I'm good. I'm not even sexually active like that. It happened once, it will not happen again. Thank you, Dr. Jones, for your time." Jasmine stormed out the room and before shutting the door she turned

back and said, "Goodbye." Dr. Jones's beautiful thick wrap bounced from side to side as she shook her head thinking, what a shame.

The silence in the car on the way home was torturing Jasmine so she turned up the radio hoping to loosen the energy in the car, but Jordan shut that attempt down quickly. She turned the radio back down and said calmly, "Jasmine, I'm going to ask some questions and if I feel like you are lying to me, all the trust I have for you will instantly vanish. Do you understand me?"

Jasmine rubbed her sweaty palms together, nervously anticipating Jordan's questions.

"Emerson told me what happened, so I'm giving you the opportunity to tell me your side." Confused, scared and speechless, Jasmine stared blankly out the window with a web of tears ready to rain in the corner of her eyes.

"You're not as innocent as I wanted you to be, that's clear. But I'm going to give you the benefit of the doubt and assume you're not as heartless as it seems." Jasmine continued to stare blankly out the window with her mouth on mute. "So, you just going to sit there and ignore me like I'm not speaking to you, Jasmine?" Jordan snapped, taking her eyes off the road for a quick second to burn Jasmine with her evil eyes. "There's no need to be hush mouth now!"

Jasmine thoughts were running a mile per hour. She silently thought, what the hell? He told her.

"Emerson told me that you got into it with some boy, and he was screaming how you was a hoe and this and that and others!"

Jasmine exhaled; she was sure that Emerson had filled Jordan's head with lies to cover his own ass, but he had only run his mouth about the incident with Travis.

"I'm going to ask you one more mother-fuckin time." Jasmine's silence aggravated Jordan's patience so, Jasmine blurted, "Travis and I got into it at the game. He's mad because I dumped him. It's like he is always trying to show out when he's around other people, so I dumped him."

Jordan cut her eyes at Jasmine then said, "So are you fucking now, Jasmine?"

"Yes, I'm fucking, okay, yes I'm fucking! Do you feel better now? But don't worry your little heart out about me. I'm using protection and no, I'm not pregnant." The tears that Jasmine had desperately tried to hold back slowly rolled down Jasmine's cheeks.

"I'm sorry, Jasmine. I just want you to know how important it is." Before Jordan could finish her sentence, Jasmine chimed in.

"I know, I know, you want me to be safe, or others to be safe or whatever. Don't worry about me, I'm fine. You've been preaching the same message since my mother died; I'm good." Jasmine was now sobbing disturbingly loud. Jordan put the car in the park and before she could reach over to comfort Jasmine; she stormed out holding her mouth. Jordan ran in after her, only to run into a puddle of roses, trailing to the beautifully decorated dinette table.

"What's this?" Jordan stopped in her trail and asked Emerson, who sat at the table with gifts bags at his feet and a cold bottle of wine to swallow down with the cooked meal he ordered,

"It's dinner. Come join me," he replied. "And to what do I owe this pleasure?" Jordan asked, pulling her a seat out at the table, instantly forgetting that Jasmine was emotionally disturbed.

"You don't owe anyone. Can't a man do something nice for his wife-to-be?"

Emerson lifted the top off the dessert platter and the beautiful, sparkling six-caret ring took the breath out of Jordan. She felt like the star of Hollywood's best flick.

"Jordan, will you be my wife?" Jordan covered her mouth with her hands; speechless, she just shook her head yes.

# 21

The sparkle from Jordan's ring glistened on the closet mirror as she struck poses like she was shooting for a Vogue cover. The diamond was beautiful from every angle and matched perfectly with the smile Jordan flashed as she realized how lucky she was.

"Do you really have to go?" Emerson asked, interrupting Jordan's quality time with her new love.

"Yes, baby, but I promise this will be the last time," she responded, wrapping her hands around his shoulders and leaning in for a kiss.

"I hope so because this shit is becoming a fucking headache. If I can't live a double life, you can't," Emerson teased Jordan. "I know, but I blew her off the entire weekend and I already promised her I would come and have a girl's night with her to make up for neglecting her. But after tonight, I'm going have to find a way to break the news to her."

Emerson presented Jordan with the side-eye. "I'm serious, even if that means letting go of our friendship. I mean, you have proved yourself, so I'm going to do the same."

Emerson frowned, wrinkling his nose. "I'll believe you when it happens," he joked, leaning in for another wet kiss from Jordan.

"Thank you for your patience baby." Jordan trailed Emerson's neck with moist kisses.

"Don't try and sweeten me up because you know you wrong. I feel like the woman who's been manipulated," Jordan said as she and Emerson both burst into laughter at his joke.

Vanilla scented candles and fresh paint fragranced Brianna's new condo.

"You can leave your shoes at the door," Brianna said to Jordan. "I was just making your favorite: baked spaghetti, fried corn, and salad." Jordan's eyes orbited the condo. She couldn't believe how good Brianna was doing financially without Emerson.

"How much you rent this a month?" Jordan was anxious to get in Brianna's business, and Brianna had no problem with flaunting her independence.

"Oh, I don't rent, this is mine. I bought it," Brianna cockily answered. "And how the hell did you buy a condo downtown?" Jordan asked, pulling out a stool at the granite island. "Oh, I'm not a fool, honey; I wasn't going to be left broke with a broken heart. It's either one or the other. Momma didn't raise a fool."

Flaunting her independence to Jordan made Brianna feel empowered. For the first time in years, Brianna wasn't crying on Jordan's shoulders or being looked down on. She noticed the envy in Jordan's eyes, and it fed her ego, so she continued to flex it. "Did you see my new ride, honey, in

the parking deck?" Brianna asked before taking the spaghetti out of the oven.

"No, I didn't see it. What kind of car you got, honey?"

Jordan's envy was loud and even she had noticed it, but she couldn't understand why she was feeling a type of way about Brianna's happiness.

"I just got a new Toyota Camry. I'm telling you now, I got too much to be blessed for and I'm now realizing that." In her silk pajamas, Brianna strutted around the new kitchen while treasure watched, and it was evident that Brianna was entering a better space in her life.

Brianna's growth was bittersweet to Jordan because a part of her felt like Brianna's happiness was a slap in her face for her betrayal.

The other part of her felt relief that Brianna might be more accepting of her and Emerson if she had truly moved on.

"Well, I'm happy you're in a better space now," Jordan added, sipping on the Moscato Brianna had poured for her. "I got to admit, I didn't think you would get over Emerson that quick," Jordan teased.

"Girl, you didn't? Shit, I didn't think I would, but I prayed about it and asked God to take the pain away and slowly with time, it's been happening. I haven't been thinking about Emerson because I know who he really is a selfish man who can never love anybody more than he loves himself."

Jordan nodded her head, but it wasn't because she agreed with Brianna. He is capable of loving, she secretly thought, you just weren't the woman for him to love.

"Stepping back from our relationship, my eyes see what my heart couldn't. Emerson is all for himself and you were right. The best thing

God could have done for me was to take him out of my life." Jordan sat silent while Brianna preached all night about being over Emerson. And for a couple of hours, Jordan bought Brianna being over Emerson. That's until she realized Brianna made him the topic of every discussion. All night Brianna talked about Emerson: the good, the bad, and his sex.

"Man don't you touch me," Jasmine snapped at Emerson, jerking his hands away from her butt. "You weren't stunning me yesterday; don't be interested in me today." Emerson pulled Jasmine in towards him by her waist. "Why were you crying anyway?" he asked, pressing his steel against her soft bottom. "Why did you have to tell her what happened at the gym?" Jasmine turned around to face Emerson and he drowned her with his clammy kisses. Instantly, she forgot why she was mad and chimed in.

Emerson lifted her up on the kitchen counter and made love to her face like she was his one and only love. "Why you got to marry her?" Jasmine murmured in between kisses. "Stop talking and fuck my brains out," Emerson demanded, pulling her *Hello Kitty* nightgown over her head. "It's not going to stop what me and you got going on, so don't worry about her. Just worry about what me and you got going on."

Emerson had quoted the oldest line for the comfort of a side chick into Jasmine's ears, and she fell for it. The anger she felt towards him the night before had instantly disappeared. "You're not like them. You're different and as soon as you get old enough, I'm going to make you mine," he whispered into her ears while she massaged his growing dick.

"Fuck me until I'm crying for you to stop, Emerson." Jasmine knew Emerson was into kinky sex and because she knew her Aunt Jordan would never give it to him like he craved, she wanted to be the one to grant him his desire, even if it killed her. Jasmine's ass was just recovering from the wild nights she and Emerson had, but she didn't care. She was going to give him all of her, including anus if he wanted it.

"You know what I want," he said after molesting Jasmine's mouth and itty-bitty breasts. "Turn over." Jasmine obeyed and turned over on her knees doggy style with her ass tooted in the air. Emerson then spread her cheeks and blew his cool breath down the crack of her ass. Her nerves were all over the place. Jasmine feared the pain that was about to come, but she wanted badly to please Emerson's every desire, so she reached her fingers back and fingered her ass.

Emerson watched her finger-fuck herself until his dick was good and hard, then without warning, he stood on the kitchen stool Jordan used to reach the back of the cabinets, and aggressively shoved his dick into Jasmine's ass.

"Ahh!" she screamed with tears raining from her eyes.

"Oh, don't cry now. You wanted this shit, remember?" Emerson didn't bother showing mercy. He loved making Jasmine pay for her decisions. He took his Mandingo and shoved as far in her ass as he could. The sound of his balls slapping against her butt cheeks and crying echoed throughout the house. "Who do you belong to little bitch?" Emerson speeds up his strokes and Jasmine's ass bounced like Jell-O.

"It's yours, Emerson, I'm yours." Emerson tested Jasmine strength and moaned the three words he knew she wanted to hear. "I love you, Jasmine. Ooh baby girl, I love you." Jasmine licked her tears from her lips then reached around and pulled Emerson in deeper into her ass by his ass.

"You deserve to have all of me, Daddy, take it," she

said as his large stick pushed deeper into her ass, making her moan even louder. "So, I can have all of you, baby?" he asked softly, playing on her weakness.

"Yes, Emerson. You know I'll give you whatever baby." Emerson slipped his dick out of Jasmine's ass then flipped her over so she could suck her juices off.

Emerson fucked Jasmine until her pussy was dry and raw. He couldn't get enough of the control he had. How he could do whatever he desired, for as long as he desired. He felt like a kid in the candy store with no rules.

# 22

Emerson and his best friend Nick neck had permanent swivels of the neck. Paranoid about their surroundings, they made sure that no one was watching them or plotting on a come up from their luxury. After ten minutes of waiting, Jasmine finally came strutting through the back alley. She strung her eyes for a better view of the black escalade.

"It's me, Jasmine! Emerson," he yelled out the window, waving his hand. "Oh, I thought that was you, but I wasn't sure whose truck this was, and I thought aunt was picking me up." Jasmine jumped in the truck.

"Oh, she told me to pick you up. She doesn't know when she and Brianna will be getting back," Emerson answered. "Oh, this is my friend, Nick, baby." Nick smiled and nodded his head from the back seat.

"Hey Nick," Jasmine said, fastening her seat belt.

"She prettier than I imagined," Nick added.

"Yeah, I told you my baby was better than yours." Jasmine blushed at Emerson's compliment.

"He going to try and tell me that his girl looked and fuck better than mine," Emerson said to Jasmine.

"Well we know that's a lie, but Emerson, you can't go yet. I'm waiting on Kira to get back with my bag. It got all my stuff in it," Jasmine said.

"Where she went?" Emerson asked.

"To the store to pick up some things. I didn't expect to be leaving so early."

Emerson looked down at his watch then said, "It's not early, it's going on ten, girl, but we'll wait a little minute." Emerson turned the car off and unbuckled his seat belt. The three of them sat quietly for a long awkward three minutes, then Emerson finally broke the silence.

"Baby, can we show him how we better?"

Jasmine's heart dropped to her stomach. A part of her knew it was coming, she just wanted to be wrong.

"Show him how?" Jasmine asked rubbing her sweaty palms together.

"Show him why you're my girl. I been bragging about you, and I don't think he believes me."

"Hell no, I don't believe you. There's no way in hell little Shawty pussy is as good as you say she is. She still got milk on her tongue," Nick added.

"We don't have to show him as long as we know, what's going on." Jasmine wanted badly to jump out of the truck, but she didn't have the courage. She watched Emerson release his dick out of the corner of her eyes. It stood straight up out his pants.

"Quit playing, Jasmine, and come suck this dick," he demanded. At that moment Jasmine wanted to cry but she didn't want to show fear. She felt betrayed by Emerson like all the other boys she had been with in school.

"Come on now, I don't have all day."

Jasmine slowly unsnapped her seat belt, leaned over, and started suckling on his earlobe. couldn't think of one thing to get her out of the situation, so she prayed that someone would happen to walk down the back alley her chance of that happening was slim to none. She peeked back at Nick out of the corner of her eye, and noticed he had his phone positioned and ready to record.

Jasmine fixated her eyes back to Emerson and she could tell that his body was yearning for her. It was the only thing that made the moment worth it. The thought of Emerson yearning for Jasmine was the only comfort space she had to get her through whatever that was about to happen. She slid her tongue from Emerson's ear to his neck, sucking on him like a lollipop.

"Um," he groaned.

The thought of what was about to go down had Emerson feeling for Jasmine big time. He could hardly wait, so he pushed Jasmine's head down to his dick and she deep throated his entire dick. "Oh, hell yeah, little momma, suck that shit then," Nick said with his phone positioned to capture the oral.

Emerson wanted to show off his control, so he shoved Jasmine head down as he fucked his dick deeper into Jasmine's mouth. He didn't have a care in the world about Jasmine gagging. When he pulled his steel out of her mouth, he slid it across her lips, rubbing the saliva all over her face.

"Suck him like you mean it, baby girl." Nick smacked his hands across Jasmine's ass so hard it echoed.

She knew then it was going to be a long night. She sucked Emerson's dick for endless minutes, caressing his balls all at once. Finally, Emerson shot a hot load of cum into her mouth.

"Did you get that, bra?" Emerson asked Nick who had the camera in Jasmine's Jasmine face as she flaunted the seeds on her tongue like the porn stars.

"Oh yeah, I got that, all that," he responded, pulling Jasmine's dress up over her waist, sliding his hands up and down the crack of her ass. "Emerson, you know what I want." Nick softly slid his two fingers into Jasmine's ass and tears began to roll down her face.

"You want me to stop, baby?" he asked after noticing her tears. Before she could reply, Emerson said, "Naw, she always cries when you get to her favorite spot." Emerson stuck four of his fingers into her ass.

"No Emerson!" she finally screamed out.

"Shut up, bitch." Emerson ass-fucked Jasmine faster and harder. "Turn the camera off, bra," Emerson demanded.

"She thinks I'm playing with her ass." Emerson spread Jasmine ass cheeks then demanded Nick, "Put your fist in this bitch's ass." With no hesitation, Nick shoved four of his fingers into Jasmine ass while Emerson kept her cheeks spread wide open.

"Yo, who is that over there looking in the truck and shit, Emerson?" Nick asked, pointing at the wino by the dumpster.

"Man, that ain't nobody but a drunk. Fuck that, let's fuck this bitch until her ass falls out." And Emerson and Nick did just that. The two of them fucked Jasmine in the back seat of the truck until she couldn't produce any more juice. Her ass and vagina were dry and sore, and her

mouth was numb from sucking both their dicks on and off. Emerson was aware of the damage, so he was up all up for damage control.

After he dropped Nick off, Jasmine and Emerson went out for dinner, and he whispered in her ear how much he loved her and how she was going to be the mother of his kids one day. Like a toddler who craves candy, she ate it. Jasmine was more in love with Emerson after the rape than before.

She knew if she kept granting Emerson's wishes, she would eventually win him over and she would finally be blessed with a family of her own one day. A family she could love unconditionally.

Being Emerson's puppy was part of the sacrifice. That's what Jasmine silently told herself on their way home when she felt like crying. She concluded she would do it all over again if she had to because she wasn't going to risk losing her aunt and not leave with her trophy. Emerson sped through the rain, trying to make it home. He knew that he and Jasmine had been out too long and the last thing he needed was Jordan getting suspicious.

Despite his actions over the past weeks, Emerson was very much in love with Jordan, and he couldn't stomach her knowing about him and Jasmine being involved. He pressed the pedal to the floor after looking down at his watch. It was going on twelve o'clock and he desperately needed to get home. But luck wasn't quite on his side. The police blue lights whipped up behind him, demanding that he pull over.

# 23

The thick green veins in Brianna's neck looked like snakes corrupting her from the inside. Her trembling legs shook the dinette table as she listened silently to the caller on the other end of the phone. Jordan knew from Brianna's mean mug that the news had to be big and disturbing. She just prayed it wasn't what she thought it was. Jordan wanted to be the one to tell Brianna about her affair with Emerson, but her intuition and Brianna's look said that she may be a little too late for the first slice of pie.

Jordan could feel the heat from Brianna's eyes burning a hole through her skin, so she waited patiently for Brianna to get off the phone while she secretly thought of some answers to the questions she knew were coming. "And you are a hundred percent sure it was her, Roxanne?" Brianna calmly asked her mother. "Oh right, I did hear enough. Let me call you back."

Jordan's guts boiled like she was in court about to face a judge. "Oh, right momma, I hear you. I got Jordan right here now. Let me talk to her and I'll call you back." Jordan sipped her Moscato, pretending to be anxious for the news. "You know you need to start spilling. You have had me in suspense for too long. What's going on?"

Brianna ignored Jordan's question, deliberately keeping her in suspense for over three minutes to see if Jordan would crack under the pressure. However, Jordan's remained composed and sat at the table, looking confused and lost like a clueless dog.

"So, this is why you been so calm about me and Emerson splitting up?" Brianna finally said to Jordan.

"What?" Jordan tooted her nose and her left eyebrow rose like she was a Rock ole lady.

"Look, bitch, don't beat around the bush with me; if you got something to say, say it, and make it clear," Jordan snapped with increased volume. "So, you are telling me you don't know?" Brianna quickly changed her tone once she noticed Jordan's frustration.

"Known what, Brianna? I don't have time to play games with your ass!" Brianna took a good look into Jordan's eyes then concluded she really was clueless. "Shit, Jordan. I don't know how to say this so I'm just going to say it."

Jordan's thoughts were scattered everywhere like puzzle pieces. She couldn't figure out what it was exactly that Brianna had to tell her. Initially, she thought Brianna was about to come at her about her and Emerson's affair, but

Brianna's actions and choice of words weren't quite leading toward that accusation.

"Emerson and Jasmine are fucking around."

Finally, Jordan exhaled like she had no worries until she realized she needed to play the denial role. "Girl, I thought you had something to tell me; clearly you don't because that's some bullshit you are talking."

Brianna shook her head, took another sip of her Moscato then finally responded, "I knew you weren't going to believe me. When are you going to wake up, Jordan? Jasmine is fucking everything with a dick!"

Jordan wasn't quite in the blind about Jasmine being sexually active, but she knew for sure it wasn't with Emerson. She couldn't tell Brianna how she knew for certain that Jasmine wasn't sleeping with Emerson.

"I'm not blind about her having sex, Brianna. She tells me everything, but for you to think she is having an affair with Emerson... I mean, come on, that's just below the belt." Like a good actress, Jordan formed a web of tears in the corners of her eyes.

"I'm not trying to hurt you, Jordan."

"You have been here for me through too much, like for real, you're like a sister to me. But Roxanne just saw Jasmine and Emerson in the truck together, parked outside in a cut in Mechanicville."

On the inside Jordan was laughing. She knew that she had shot a text to Emerson earlier to pick up Jasmine from her friend's house, but she couldn't quite tell Brianna that without blowing her cover.

"Roxanne said she saw them from the alley, fucking in the truck," Brianna added.

"This is Roxanne we are talking about here, Brianna. Are you hearing yourself right now?" Jordan barked. "My momma may be a lot of things, but a liar isn't one of them, Jordan. You swear that your family is so much better, but the reality is yawl shit smells just like everybody else's, boo." Brianna banged her hands on the dinette table.

"I never said my family was better; them your words, so clearly that's what you think Brianna." Jordan began pacing the living area searching for her things.

"So, you're telling me you think Emerson would fuck a fourteen-year-old girl? Do you think your man can fuck a child because, I mean, I hated the bastard, but I didn't get that vibe from him at all? So please give me your input Ms. Know-it-all."

Brianna's heart caved in. She knew the truth was killing Jordan deep down inside, and as a friend, she just wanted to comfort her. But the other half of her wanted to inform Jordan about the little devil she held close to her heart.

"Yes, if you really want to know the truth about it, yes, I think, in fact, I know Emerson would fuck a teen. It wouldn't be his first time either." Brianna's words were like fire to Jordan's skin. Instantly her body was covered in warmth; Jordan's body began trembling and her motherly concern started to drown her thoughts.

*Do you know him as well as you think you know him? Has he ever looked at her funny? Don't trip, Jordan, you know what's going on. How you gon' let them tell you otherwise.*

"Well, all I can do is ask Jasmine. She would tell me the truth," Jordan responded.

"Well, if you need me, I will be here; just let me know."

"I'm good, I got it; I'll get it under control."

Brianna shook her head in shame, thinking it was just like Jordan to pretend to have everything under control when it came for her to need a shoulder to lean on.

"You don't have to pretend to be superwoman all the time, Jordan." Jordan held her hand up, requesting that Brianna keep quiet so she could answer her phone.

"Hello," Jordan answered.

"Aunt, you got to go and get Uncle Emerson out of jail! He's been arrested with a warrant," Jasmine sobbed loudly on the phone.

"What?" Jordan snapped.

"They just locked him up for a warrant, and they reported the truck because I was too young to drive it."

The tables had flipped and now Brianna was curiously waiting for Jordan to get off the phone to ask her what was going on.

"Where are you, Jasmine?" Jordan screamed in the phone.

"I'm at the bus stop. I asked the police if I could catch the bus home since I wasn't that far. He said yes after I started crying, but at first, he was trying to take me to children's services."

Jordan snatched up her Chanel tote bag and stormed out the door, before slamming the door behind her she turned to Brianna and said, "Oh, I'll call you later; I got to go."

# 24

The four walls felt like they were caving in on Emerson and his ears were ringing like a grenade had been thrown into the holding cell with him. He sat on the bench in a rage for hours, impatiently rocking back and forth, waiting to be bailed out.

Fortunately for Emerson, his bail didn't get revoked after he jumped on the two guards who treated him like the scum beneath their shoes. Having money had really come in handy for Emerson. He knew the sergeant who eventually convinced the guards he jumped on not to press charges.

Jordan's nerves were shocked, and her heart was heavy. She felt for Emerson; she imagined he was losing his mind, sitting in a cell enraged at Brianna for pressing charges against him, and the sticky part about the whole thing was Jordan knew about the entire situation. She was fully aware that Brianna had pressed charges on Emerson, but she kept quiet about it so he wouldn't blow her cover by exposing to Brianna that he knew.

Jordan sat irritably in the bondman's office Emerson's homeboy Nick had recommended, wobbling her legs and biting down on her bottom lip, sincerely praying for them to speed up the process.

"Ms. Brown," the bonds lady Ms. Patricia Walker called out.

"Yes?" she answered quickly, strutting to Ms. Walker's desk.

"I just need to ask you some questions and we can get this thing on the road. Are you and Mr. Waters married?" Patricia's eyes were glued to the papers. She never looked at Jordan.

"No, not yet" Jordan answered.

"Okay, that's fine. Has he ever been locked up before?" Jordan wasn't sure and didn't want to lie, so she just shoved her shoulders with attitude. When Ms. Walker didn't hear her response, she looked up at Jordan and repeated the question. "Has he ever been locked up before? Does he have any other bails pending?" Irritated, Jordan shoved her shoulders up and down again.

"Hey, don't I know you from somewhere?" Patricia asked, changing the subject.

"No, I don't think so," Jordan answered.

"I swear you look familiar, girl. What side of town you from?" Jordan wished to the gods that Patricia had just done her job and kept the conversation short, but that wasn't happening.

"I'm from Atlanta. You might have seen me around those areas, but how long will this take before he is released? Jordan attempted to change the subject, but Patricia was more into girl talk than work. She brushed Jordan's question off with a short response.

"Oh, this won't take long. He'll be out in a minute. Don't worry about that." Jordan wanted more details, like what's a minute exactly and when would he have to go to court on the charges, but Patricia just resumed with the girl talk.

"Where did you get that from, girl? That mother fucker is bad." Jordan fed Patricia's curiosity with silence.

"Oh, let me give you a copy of the papers. I'm just running my mouth," she said after realizing that Jordan wasn't up for girl talk. "I swear you look like this girl I know. She got the same hazel eyes just like you. I thought you were her for a minute." Jordan flashed her fake smile and intolerantly waited for her to finish copying the paperwork.

"Okay, sign your name right here for me." Patricia read Jordan's name and the light flicked on in her head. She murmured, "Oh," on the way back to the copier.

"Well, he should be released in the next couple of hours depending on how long Rice Street jail take to process him out. We can give you a call when he's been released, or you can go to Rice St. yourself and pressure them to move faster."

Patricia stapled a load of papers together then handed them to Jordan, who immediately stormed out the door as soon as the papers hit her hands.

# 25

R-Kelly's *Feeling on Your Booty* didn't do anything for the awkward mood in the seven forty-five; the tension was so sharp you could cut a finger.

Jordan had attempted to make conversation with Emerson, but it was an epic fail every time. She said at least three (are you okay?) to six words (where did the warrant come from?) to Emerson, but he didn't give her one word in return. Jordan wasn't sure if Emerson knew she was aware of his warrant or if he was just generally pissed. So, she kept quiet and focused on the rainy road ahead.

And like an unexpected decrease in the weather when you got a cold, Brianna's name flashed across Jordan's phone. She quickly attempted to silence the phone, but it hopped around in the drink holder like a free rabbit, causing her mission to take longer than she had wished.

Jordan cupped the cellular in between her thighs for better access, then glanced over at Emerson to check if he was fazed by the call. She got no answer. His face had no expression, which was scary because his aura screamed: "don't fuck with me."

Jordan's phone began ringing again, and every time she silenced it Brianna would call right back, and right back, and right back. So, she

figured it would be less disturbing to answer the call then it will be to continue to ignore it. "Hello," Jordan murmured.

"You know what? I knew it was something when I smelled his stinky-ass cologne on you last night!" Brianna yelled into the phone. "You were my friend—more like my sister, bitch! How could you fuck the man I loved?!"

Jordan's eyes browsed over at Emerson to see if he could hear Brianna yelling through the phone.

"What the hell you are talking about, bitch?" Jordan muttered. "You know what the fuck I'm talking about! You're fucking Emerson! My home girl just called and told me that you just bailed Emerson out of jail." Jordan could feel Brianna's pain through her sobbing outburst. "Girl, you all hysterical for nothing. You don't know what the hell you're talking about."

Jordan tried her best to remain calm; the timing was all wrong and she knew Emerson wasn't in the mood for the drama, especially from Brianna since she was the one who was responsible for his arrest. "I'll call you when

I get home because this is not the time. I'm driving and it's raining like hell out here."

"Just answer one question for me Jordan... How long has this being going on?" Brianna waited for an answer for two long minutes crying her heart out. "How long, Jordan?!" she snapped.

"I told you this is not the time, Brianna."

Emerson snatched the phone from Jordan's ear and snapped, "Bitch, if you knew what was good for you, you would hang up this phone and disappear."

Jordan's heart could have flown out of her chest; she was so nervous and scared of the drama that was about to unfold. "I'm not scared of you, punk-ass nigga. Out of all the bitches in the world you had to take the only somebody I had... Emerson!" Emerson listened silently to Brianna while she poured her frustration out on the table thick.

"I loved you. I've never done anything to hurt you, Emerson. I gave you the best part of me and you go and make my best friend my enemy." Everything ain't what it seems; just be blessed that you made out, Brianna."

Jordan glanced at Emerson to see where he was coming from with his comment, and for the first time ever she saw remorse in his eyes for Brianna. She snatched the phone back from Emerson immediately; she couldn't afford to lose him at the very moment she was losing her best friend.

"Brianna, I get that you're mad and if you're interested, we can sit down and talk and I promise you I will answer whatever you want me to answer, but this is not a good time," Jordan said.

"Bitch, God don't like ugly and you one ugly bitch. And you can say whatever you want to say about my mother but one thing, she is not is a liar and she wasn't lying when she said that Jasmine and Emerson were fucking in the truck." Emerson could hear Brianna's accusations through the phone, so he reached over to Jordan, attempting to end the call. Jordan snatched away from him. "So, I guess in the end, I wasn't the one to get the short end of the stick. Ha, the jokes on you, bitch!"

Jordan's heart caved. She secretly prayed that Roxanne had her facts wrong, but her intuition told her otherwise. Jordan was somewhat speechless; all she can say was, "Girl, you know what, I can't deal with this shit right now."

"Yeah, you don't ever want to hear the truth, but the jokes on you. You played pussy and got fucked, bitch!"

Though Brianna's words were harsh and hard to the core, Jordan could still hear the pain between the sniffles.

"I love you, Brianna, goodbye." Jordan tossed her phone into her purse then looked over to Emerson with the evil eye.

"Look, you better not question me about shit that bitch told you! She pissed and hurt and wants you to join the club, and frankly, I'm not in the mood for the bullshit. Plus, we got some shit to talk about when we get home." Emerson didn't bother speaking on what he wanted to talk to Jordan about. After asking him four times what was on his mind, she finally gave up and decided to wait until they got home to hear him out.

# 26

Emerson's silence had Jordan's nerves shuddering, her trembling hands blindly searched through her Jessica Simpson bag for the keys to the door, and after three long minutes, Jordan finally got the door opened.

"Baby, do you want me to fix you something to..."

Before Jordan could finish speaking, she felt a forceful blow to the back of her head. She dropped her bag and her personal belongings scattered all over the floor. Jordan attempted to face Emerson, but before she could turn around, he banged her head into the kitchen granite.

"Bitch, I ought to kill you, hoe! Bitch, you put my life in danger!" Confused, Jordan pressed her hand tightly on the pain in the back of her head and yelled out, "What the fuck are you talking about Emerson?" All her sobbing didn't matter. He ignored her question and continued to pound on her face like it was his personal punching bag. "Bitch, I thought you was differentAnd to think I wanted to marry you." Jordan couldn't get a word into Emerson. His rage was too strong. He slung Jordan from one side of the house to the other; it was entirely too much racket for Jasmine to sleep through. She ran downstairs at the sound of the shattered glass to see what was going on.

"Get off her. What are you doing?" Jasmine ran down the stairs like she was running in the Olympics. "What the fuck is wrong with you? Why are you hitting her?" Jasmine struggled to untangle Emerson's hands from Jordan's hair. It was so much she couldn't stomach. Jordan's face was swollen worse than Rocky's after a fight.

"This bitch has ruined my life!" he continued to yell out, smashing his feet into her ribs.

"Stop, Emerson, please! Just tell me what you're mad about!" Jordan wept.

"I'm calling the fucking police on you!" Jasmine took off upstairs to fetch her phone.

"You gave me HIV, bitch!" Emerson blurted, jacking Jordan up on the wall.

"What?" Jordan kneed Emerson in his dick. He kneeled and moaned.

"Aww, you bitch!"

"So, it's true? How could you, you dirty motherfucker!" Jordan balled her fist up and pounded Emerson's face as hard as she could while he was still kneeling. "How dare you, bitch! Come in here putting your fucking hands on me, when you're the fucking one who's been up to no good the entire time!"

Jordan began kickboxing Emerson's ribs, screaming, "Jasmine, Jasmine, come here!"

Jasmine jumped at the sound of Jordan's voice and immediately ran to her rescue.

"I'm coming, aunt, here I come," she yelled on her way to the living area.

"What the fuck are you talking about?" Emerson growled out, still holding his balls.

"What I'm talking about?" Jordan repeated. "I'm talking about how you two mother fuckers have been fucking up under my roof!" Jasmine froze in her footsteps, standing still at the bottom of the stairs.

"I haven't been fucking no Jasmine, bitch!" Emerson swung but he missed. Jordan's good one eye had seen his blow coming before he swung.

"Yes, you have, bitch. That's who gave you the fucking HIV. She's been HIV positive since birth. Her mother gave it to her."

Jasmine stood speechless with tears pouring from her beautiful hazel eyes.

"You thought you were winning. You thought you had yourself a pretty mixed redbone to call your own. Ha!" Jordan uttered out. Emerson was stunned. Not only was he embarrassed for Jordan to know what he had been up to, but he was pissed beyond measure that he played himself short. "My sister died of AIDS, or did you forget that I told you that, dummy?" Tears rushed down Jordan's bruised cheeks.

"I guess karma is a bitch and we're the suckers. You played Russian roulette with hearts and got the bad end of the stick." Jasmine stared at her aunt, thinking silently, I'm so sorry aunt.

"Silly Jordan for thinking she won something special." Jordan was soaked in so much pain. She didn't feel an ache from her left hand that pounded across her chest. "Look at me, Jasmine. How could you do this to me, Jasmine! How could you put my life in danger like this?" Jasmine stepped backward up the stairs as Jordan walked closer to her.

"I didn't put your life in danger; he raped me after you stopped giving him sex."

Jordan took off towards Jasmine.

"So, you're safe!" she blurted before running further up the stairs. "Why didn't you tell me he did that to you, Jasmine?"

"Because I didn't rape that bitch, she seduced me! That little hoe been fucking everything with a dick!" Emerson exclaimed.

"You know what? You two motherfuckers can have each other." Plaw! Jasmine gripped on to her stinging face. "If he raped you, you should have told me, so that's on you," Jordan screamed after slapping the living daylights out of Jasmine.

"And that's what your punk ass gets for fucking, shoving your dick inside a fucking teenager; you fucking disgust me. She's a fucking child, for God's sake!" Jordan snatched her wallet up off the floor and stormed out the door.

# 27

---

Emerson was like the lion and Jasmine was prey. He could smell her fear. She stood trembling on the bottom step, contemplating on what move to make. She couldn't believe her aunt left her to fend for herself towards a man who was clearly in a rage.

"You young stupid bitch," Emerson finally yelled, pacing towards Jasmine. "You ruined my mother fucking life!" Jasmine took off up the stairs. She attempted to lock herself in the bedroom, but she was unsuccessful. Emerson pushed the door open behind her then forcefully tossed her onto the bed.

"Bitch, you knew the entire time you were infected. That's why you seduced me!" Emerson yelled out, ripping Jasmine's silk gown off her.

"I didn't try to give it to you, I swear. Please don't hurt me, Emerson!" she sobbed out before Emerson's fist pounded into her mouth. "Ouch, please Emerson!" Jasmine struggled with blocking her face with her forearm. Every time she put her arms up, Emerson would remove them and strike her again.

"Bitch, don't you know they lock people up for knowingly passing that shit around to people!" Jasmine's loose breasts wobbled from side to side. Emerson beat Jasmine with her nude body on display. There wasn't

Jasmine crying meant nothing to Emerson. He slapped her hands against her butt cheeks and demanded, "Keep them spread, bitch, or it's going to be a long night." Jasmine obeyed his command, hoping it would speed the process. Emerson shoved his entire dick deep into her ass. His balls were the only part of his stick that was free, and they slammed against her ass cheeks as he dug in a circular motion, attempting to hit her every wall.

"Aww, please, I'm dry!" she screamed.

The more Jasmine exposed her pain, the more pleasure Emerson reaped. Her tears brought him comfort. He wanted her to feel the pain he was feeling, and so far, he was succeeding. He took the tube and slid it in and out of Jasmine's vagina.

The cool glass felt weird, and it even tickled Jasmine a little until Emerson found the right rhythm. He slid the glass in and out faster and faster. The deeper and more aggressive he got with the tube; the more nervous Jasmine became. She feared the glass would break into her vagina. Emerson shoved both his dick and the tube into Jasmine's holes with force, groaning out loud, "Aww, shit, yes, fuck you, bitch!" The words Emerson moaned made no sense, but they felt good to him.

He felt powerful with every stroke he dug into Jasmine. Not caring about being safe, Emerson shot his warm semen into Jasmine's ass then watched it drip out of her ass like a waterfall. "Bitch since I can't fuck anybody else, you're going to be my sex slave."

Emerson flipped over flat on his back, lying next to Jasmine in the twin bed. "Here, suck your pussy juices off this tube," he said with the tube sliding across Jasmine's lips. "What are you doing, bitch? It's not time for you to sleep." Emerson grabbed Jasmine by the head and tossed it towards his Mandingo.

"Kiss on my dick until it's hard again," he demanded, closing his eyes, waiting for his treat.

Jasmine obeyed Emerson's order and made love to his dick and massaged his balls.

When she felt like he was good and comfortable, she kneed him so hard he could feel the pain in his stomach. Jasmine ran for her life, naked and free out on the dark streets of Atlanta.

# 28

---

Jasmine's flat, narrow feet crushed the grits and rocks on the cold pavement, and her breasts wobbled free as she ran down the dark road. There was not a soul in sight. It was the wee hours, the hours when only eighteen-wheelers traveled the streets. Bummmmmmmmmp! The loud farmer truck blew before pulling over.

"Sweetheart, where you going? You, okay?" the bare mouth snuff-sniffing elder yelled out the window.

"Can you please take me to the police station?" Jasmine bawled out.

"Yeah, sweetheart, come on," he answered, pulling over to the curve.

Jasmine hopped in the truck without a second thought. Her heart was racing, and her nerves were shattered. She was scared for her life and just wanted to get out of Emerson's reach.

"Now where you say you going, sweetheart?" the grey-bearded trucker asked.

"Just take me to the police station, please." Jasmine wiped her tears from her eyes then asked, "Can I please put on your coat?" She eyed the farmer's coat beneath his butt and prayed he would have sympathy towards her and give it to her with no problem.

"Well, darling, I need that coat, but what are you doing out here without any clothes?"

The trucker's eyes fixated on Jasmine's young beautiful body. She just sobbed, hoping he would soften up and say yes, but he didn't change his answer—just his actions. He couldn't help himself. He rubbed his hands softly down her thighs and said, "I'll give you what you want if you give me what I want."

Jasmine looked over at the old man who was old enough to be her grandfather and said, "I can't give you anything, just let me out, please!" The trucker ignored Jasmine and continued to the highway.

"Sweetie, I can't let you out yet, you have to wait until we get off the highway. This is a big truck. I just can't stop like that."

The trucker whose uniform read "Rodger" drove deep into the expressway, then pulled over to a rest spot. Jasmine's heart dropped; she knew it couldn't be good.

"Why are you stopping?" she sobbed.

"Baby, you were sent to me from God," he said, rubbing on Jasmine's Jasmine nipples.

"Stop, don't touch me," she screamed.

"Baby you can scream all you want, but no one can hear you. Besides, this won't take long. As good as you are looking, this won't take long." Jasmine covered her breasts with one hand and her sore vagina with the other. "I got HIV, you better not touch me, I'm telling you!" Jasmine screamed out in her defense. "Baby, I'm sixty-seven years old. Even if that was true, it wouldn't hurt me. I don't have that damn long anyway." Rodger leaned in and sucked on Jasmine's neck. He could tell she had already been raped from the smell of sex that fragranced her body, and her

bruised swollen face that her innocent tears showered down from, but he couldn't resist. Her body was like chocolate to a fat kid on a diet. Jasmine pulled and tussled to get Rodger off her, and after losing his patience, Rodger reached into the dashboard and pulled out his gun. "Bitch, you move one more time, I will shoot your ass and toss you out on this highway."

Jasmine sobbed louder, but she didn't pull away anymore. She allowed old man Rodger to suck on her itty-bitty breast like she was the love of his life.

"Aww, baby girl, you are so beautiful," he said, spreading her legs open so he could taste her desert.

"Come on, open up. Let me show how a real man feels." Rodger slid his tongue up and down Jasmine's sore vagina and to her surprise, it felt soothing. She then opened a little wider, allowing him access to dig his tongue deeper.

"Aww, little momma, I might have to take you with

me to Texas," he said, sliding his tongue in and out of her pussy hole gently. "Um, you taste like fine wine," he murmured before shoving his face all in her cherry pie. "Just tell me you like it even if you don't. I promise it'll help me get my victory quicker."

Tears poured from Jasmine's face. She couldn't believe her day. Most of all, she couldn't believe what she was about to partake in and why. She moaned out, "Aww, Daddy, I been waiting for you to eat this pussy."

Rodger's pace picked up. He ate the pie like he was in a pie-eating contest with no time to spare. He shook his head all in her juices, then kissed and sucked her clitoris like it was his long-time wife's pussy he was eating.

"Aww, it's time for Daddy to put this dick in you," he whispered before ripping off his belt buckle and pulling down his pants.

"Fuck me, Daddy, fuck me."

Jasmine's tears increased. She was content with being taken advantage of. She had no more energy to fight. She lay flat back on the seat with her head resting on the door, waiting for old man Rodger to fuck her lights out. He took the head of his dick and first slid it down her clitoris.

"Girl, God sent you to me; he knew my dick was craving to please you." As sick as he sounded, Jasmine believed him.

She figured it had to be God's plan. Why else would he send her to Rodger? She grabbed his old, wrinkled dick and shoved it into her sore vagina.

"Fuck me already," she moaned out, ready for it to be over with.

"Aww!" Rodger could barely take it. He hadn't had any pussy in five years and Jasmine's was too good to be true. He was grinding slow and deep, trying to save the moment, but his old worm wasn't hearing it. Every time he made a stroke, it felt like it would be his last.

"Aww, just be patient with me baby. Please, I love you," he mumbled, and Jasmine shook her head in shame. She couldn't figure out what it was about her sex that made men do and say the craziest things. She spread her legs and pushed Rodger into her deep by his ass.

"Come on, you wanted it. Now fuck it like it's yours."

Rodger sucked on Jasmine's breast, and she cringed at his gums massaging her nipples.

"Aww, baby girl, I'm coming," he said after just three short minutes of grinding. His warm worms squirted into Jasmine, and she just burst

into tears. Her emotions were all over the place and she couldn't control them. She didn't know how to feel anymore. Rodger's dead weight rested on her chest as he rubbed her ass, praying he would get hard again. Free young pussy with easy access was just not easy to come by for a man like him.

Jasmine looked up at the ceiling of the truck, thinking... what am I going to do with my life now? After ten minutes of soaking in Rodger's sweat, Jasmine blurted out, "Come on, get up, Rodger, and take me to Texas with you. You can fuck me as long as you want, however you want, as long as you take care of me."

Jasmine's words were like Christmas gifts unwrapped. Rodger couldn't believe what he was hearing. He lifted and said, "What?"

"You heard me right; I'm all yours, baby, but I'm expensive so you better start putting in for overtime." Rodger's eyes lit up like a kid in a candy factory.

"Baby, you don't have to worry about nothing. Daddy got you." He kissed Jasmine's neck for another two minutes.

"Um, I hit the jackpot. You're so beautiful too," he crooned, drowning her nude body with his wet soggy kisses. "Daddy's going to wake up eating your pussy, shoving my tongue all in your ass."

Jasmine knew that Rodger was in desperate need of good loving. He admired her more than any man ever would since she was everything he couldn't have. She massaged and kissed on his old, scribbled dick until it was hard and sucked on it on their way to Texas. Her new plan was to use the old man Rodger for a new start in life.

No one knew her in Texas, and so she would be granted a new start, and she was going to be damn sure that Rodger blessed her with any and

everything she desired. The way he cried while she slurped on his dick was hard proof that her mission would be easier than taking candy from a baby.

# 29

The second hand on the clock turned into minutes and the minutes were working on an hour. Jordan knew a walk-in would take a large chunk out of her day, but what she couldn't prepare herself for was the horrid visuals of the doctor telling her she was HIV positive. She'd prayed for the best but the worse played with her emotions. She couldn't stop imaging the doctor telling her the bad news. She sat waiting in the backroom for the doctor to return with her test results. Her legs shook like a loose branch on a tree.

"Sorry for the wait, Ms. Brown. I know time seems to move like a snail when you're waiting for test results." Jordan flashed Dr. Huff a fake smile then replied, "You have no idea."

"Well, I'm just happy that you young girls take time out of your busy schedules to check on your health." Jordan tuned Dr. Huff out. Like always she rambled on and on about every good act under the sun.

"Are you and Ms. Braxton still best friends?" Dr. Huff asked, flipping through Jordan's paperwork.

"Yes, we're still friends," Jordan lied.

"Oh okay, that explains it, the two of you are trying to start your own pregnancy pack."

Jordan's heart dropped to her stomach at the sound of pregnancy. "Did you say pregnancy?" she asked with her left eyebrow raised and her nose tooted.

"Yes, I did, ma'am. Congratulations, you're going to be a mommy." Dr. Huff's smile warmed Jordan's heart. She had been her and Brianna's doctor since they were teens, coming to the teen clinic. "You and Ms. Braxton are in competition I see." The second hint finally hit Jordan. She picked at Dr. Huff, to get more information on Brianna's visit.

"Oh, Brianna's appointment was today. I thought it was yesterday," Jordan said, hoping Dr. Huff felt comfortable enough to spill the beans on Brianna's visit.

"Oh no, her visit was today. She just left shortly before you came."

"Well, she knew she was pregnant, me, I'm super surprised. I simply wanted to get me an HIV test done because I'm in a new relationship."

"Well, she didn't seem like she knew it, in fact, she only came in to get checked for HIV as well."

Jordan had successfully conned Dr. Huff out of confidential information; she couldn't believe that both she and Brianna were carrying Emerson's babies. The love triangle had just reached its sickest height and Jordan couldn't stomach it. She gagged with her right hand covering her mouth.

"Are you okay, Ms. Brown?" Dr. Huff asked.

"Yes, I'm fine. You never told me my results," Jordan blurted before gagging again.

"Oh, girl, you're negative. You know, if it was something, I would have come in with that news first."

Dr. Huff's young spirit is what pulled the teens and young ladies into her web. She got them to open and speak to her about anything they were concerned about.

"Oh, thank God," Jordan exhaled and said.

"Were you expecting to have something, Jordan?" Dr. Huff asked.

"No, I just recently had sex and I didn't use protection, so those nightmares got to me." Jordan was quick and smooth with the lies.

"See, that's why I tell you girls to never gamble with your life like that; the risk is not worth it at all." Jordan silently shook her head no, thinking about how close she came to having her life turned upside down.

"Excuse me, Dr. Huff, but I got to go." Jordan quickly stormed out the doctor's office. She needed fresh air and some time to soak in what her life had become in the last couple of days.

The dark red blood oozed from Emerson, sliced right down to his fingertips and then onto the hardwood floor.

His life as he knew it was slowly slipping away. Not even the loud ringing cell could save him. It was the seventh time in a row that Jordan had called Emerson, and the more he ignored her, the bigger her urge grew to speak with him.

Fifteen calls later, Jordan finally decided to give up on reaching Emerson. Right after phoning him, she tried her luck reaching out to Brianna because she felt like she wasn't going to make it without speaking

to someone. After the fourth ring, the ring right before the answer machine picks up, Brianna answered.

"What do you want, Jordan?" Brianna aggressively asked.

"I'm sorry, Brianna, please don't hang up. I need to talk to you." Jordan sobbing through the phone sounded more desperate than a homeless person begging for a dollar for a hit, and Brianna wanted to hear more of her desperate plea. So, she decided not to end the call.

"I'm listening," she answered.

"I can't find Jasmine, it's been two days," Jordan said.

"She's probably somewhere with your fiancé," Brianna replied.

"I'm sorry for hurting you, Brianna. I understand your frustration and why you want to drag me to my grave, I do. I get it, but as much as I've been there for you, I'm asking you to return the favor and be here for me, just this once."

Jordan's crying increased and Brianna knew that Jordan's cry for support was genuine. The opportunity to hurt Jordan presented itself and Brianna refused to reject it in the name of a loyal friend. No, she craved for Jordan to feel the pain she had been feeling, and she felt blessed that it didn't take as long as she anticipated it would. "Well, I don't know what you want me to do. I got my own problems to cope with, and honestly, I can't return that favor right now."

"Besides it's like you don't believe nothing nobody tells you when it comes to Jasmine, and I'm telling you, your sweet little niece is fucking the nigga you stole from me. Now because of you bitches, I will be a fucking single mother, so I'm sorry, but I can't help you." Ending their friendship when Jordan needed her, felt better than free money to Brianna.

Speechless and clueless on her next move, Jordan decided to end what she and Brianna had on a high note. She texted her phone: Once again, I'm sorry for hurting you and YES, YOU'RE RIGHT! Jasmine did sleep with

Emerson, lol, I guess you can call that my karma, but I didn't sleep with him. I decided to go celibate, lucky me. The doctor said I'm clear. He only began sleeping with Jasmine because I wasn't sleeping with him. Jasmine is the only family I have, so if you hear something about her whereabouts, please tell me., Oh, and congratulations on the baby. Maybe one day we can squash our beef and raise the kids with a better bond than we were blessed with. Yeah, that's right, I'm a single mother as well. I'm having Emerson's baby.

Jasmine slung her feet from the doctor's bed, humming Mary Mary's, Thankful. She waited patiently for the doctor to return with her prescriptions. "Okay, Ms. Rivers, I have your prescription. Now I don't have to tell you how important it is for you to take all your meds on time and to not miss an appointment, right?" the doctor named Slaughter asked Jasmine.

"Oh, you don't have to worry about that, Dr. Slaughter. I will never do to my baby what my momma did to me." Jasmine rubbed her flat abdomen, thinking about her little bundle of joy.

"Well, I hope the police find whoever mugged you. I hate how these little thugs think they can just get away with things." Dr. Slaughter could

barely stomach the lie Jasmine told her about being mugged when she asked Jasmine about the bruises on her face.

"Yeah, my granddaddy just told me to pray about it and leave it in God's hands." Jasmine didn't need an acting coach. She dove into role-playing at the sound of action.

"Yeah, Mr. Rodgers is a good man. I have known him for a minute now. I never knew he had a granddaughter, though," Dr. Slaughter responded, tearing off Jasmine's prescriptions pages.

"Yeah, I know. He didn't even know. We just found out ourselves."

"So, are you from Texas?"

"No, I'm just going to be leaving with my granddaddy for a while; at least until I and momma get back on good terms," Jasmine lied.

"I understand. Well, I'll see you back here in a week, okay?" Jasmine grabbed her prescriptions and strutted out the office like a lotto winner.

# The Winning Code

(Email this code and proof of review to Thebookplug@yahoo.com to win one of many cool prizes) (Gift cards, T-shirts, Autographed books, coffee mugs, cool bookmarks etc.)

1004

# THE END

# GUESS THE PLOT

Review on Amazon with the correct answer and email proof to thebookplug@yahoo.com for a chance to win gifts and prizes from bestselling author Cornelia Smith.... ....

➤ Do you believe the girls; Brianna, Jordan, and Jasmine will mend fences and put their problems behind them?

# KEEP IN CONTACT

## Become A VIP

➤ Text me: Cornelia to 21000

➤ Subscribe: www.thebookplug.com

➤ Email: Thebookplug@yahoo.com

➤ Facebook Group: Pretty Girls Read Gangsta shit Pretty Girls Read Gangsta Shit... Author 📧 Cornelia Smith Fan Page | Facebook

➤ Instagram:

  @Unique_butterflycs  @Thebookplug

  @AuthorCorneliaSmith

  @babyryderjanae

➤ Facebook Group: The Book Plug Fan Page | Facebook

# THE
# COLDEST
# HOE
*Ever*

*book 2*

# CORNELIA SMITH

DO YOU LIKE TO COLOR? Or KEEP BUSY WITH CROSS WORD PUZZLES? IF yes, check out some of my new entertaining, stress relieving adult coloring/activity books... & tell me what you think?

YOU GOTTA
PAY
TO PLAY
MAY YOU
Choke
ON ALL THE
Shit Your
talk
BBL
ADULT COLORING BOOK

Made in United States
Orlando, FL
02 May 2023

32710003R00093